HANDS OFF

Kenny was faster than Fargo expected. The man's right hand dropped to his holster, the .45 started gleaming in the light of the Rochester lamps and—

And in a single swift move, Fargo spun back toward the bar, grabbed the whiskey bottle by the neck and hurled it at the other man's gun hand. The bottle smashed so hard against Kenny's hand that his shot went wild as he squeezed it off. He stood there looking confused and angry, as if some diabolical magician's trick had just been played on him.

Then he made a move so dumb Fargo gave up coddling him. Drunk as he was, Kenny dove in the direction of the .45 that had been knocked from his hand and then skidded a few feet away.

Fargo had put two bullets in Kenny's gun hand before the man was even close enough to his weapon to retrieve it.

THE
TRAILSMAN

#334

COLORADO
CLASH

by

Jon Sharpe

A SIGNET BOOK

SIGNET
Published by New American Library, a division of
Penguin Group (USA) Inc., 375 Hudson Street,
New York, New York 10014, USA
Penguin Group (Canada), 90 Eglinton Avenue East, Suite 700, Toronto,
Ontario M4P 2Y3, Canada (a division of Pearson Penguin Canada Inc.)
Penguin Books Ltd., 80 Strand, London WC2R 0RL, England
Penguin Ireland, 25 St. Stephen's Green, Dublin 2,
Ireland (a division of Penguin Books Ltd.)
Penguin Group (Australia), 250 Camberwell Road, Camberwell, Victoria 3124,
Australia (a division of Pearson Australia Group Pty. Ltd.)
Penguin Books India Pvt. Ltd., 11 Community Centre, Panchsheel Park,
New Delhi - 110 017, India
Penguin Group (NZ), 67 Apollo Drive, Rosedale, North Shore 0632,
New Zealand (a division of Pearson New Zealand Ltd.)
Penguin Books (South Africa) (Pty.) Ltd., 24 Sturdee Avenue,
Rosebank, Johannesburg 2196, South Africa

Penguin Books Ltd., Registered Offices:
80 Strand, London WC2R 0RL, England

First published by Signet, an imprint of New American Library,
a division of Penguin Group (USA) Inc.

First Printing, August 2009
10 9 8 7 6 5 4 3 2 1

The first chapter of this book previously appeared in *Black Hills Badman*, the three
hundred thirty-third volume in this series.

The Trailsman

Beginnings . . . they bend the tree and they mark the man. Skye Fargo was born when he was eighteen. Terror was his midwife, vengeance his first cry. Killing spawned Skye Fargo, ruthless, cold-blooded murder. Out of the acrid smoke of gunpowder still hanging in the air, he rose, cried out a promise never forgotten.

The Trailsman they began to call him all across the West: searcher, scout, hunter, the man who could see where others only looked, his skills for hire but not his soul, the man who lived each day to the fullest, yet trailed each tomorrow. Skye Fargo, the Trailsman, the seeker who could take the wildness of a land and the wanting of a woman and make them his own.

Colorado, 1861—three men dead, a town filled with ugly secrets and Fargo trying to stay alive long enough to learn the truth.

1

Skye Fargo might not have found the body if he hadn't decided to stop by the creek and fill his canteen.

Late September in Colorado was a melancholy time with the thinness of the afternoon sunlight and the snow-peaked mountains looking cold and aloof.

Ground-tying his big Ovaro stallion, Fargo grabbed his canteen from his saddle and walked through buffalo grass until he came to the narrow, winding creek. The water was clean. He hunched down next to it, opening his canteen. A jay cried. Fargo looked over to see what the hell was wrong with the damned bird.

And that was when he saw, sticking out from behind a ponderosa pine to his right, a pair of boots. Easy to assume that attached to those boots was a body.

He finished filling his canteen before getting up and walking through the smoky air to stand over the remains of what appeared to be a teenager of maybe sixteen, seventeen years. From the denim shirt and Levi's and chaps, Fargo figured that the kid had been a drover. Cattle were getting to be a big business around here.

The birds had already been at him pretty good. The cheeks reminded Fargo of a leper he'd once seen. One of the eyes had been pecked in half. Dried blood spread over the front of the kid's shirt. Hard to tell how long the kid had been here. Fargo figured a long day at least. The three bullets had done their job.

He found papers in the kid's back pocket identifying him as Clete Byrnes, an employee of the Bar DD and a member of the Cawthorne, Colorado, Lutheran Church. Cawthorne was a good-sized town a mile north of here. That was where Fargo had been headed.

He stood up, his knees cracking, and rolled himself a smoke. He'd seen his share of death over the years and by now he was able to see it without letting it shake him. The West was a dangerous place and if bullets weren't killing people then diseases were. But the young ones got to him sometimes. All their lives ahead of them, cut down so soon.

The cigarette tasted good, the aroma killing some of the stench of the kid's body.

Not far away was a soddie. He walked toward it and called out. Then he went to the door but there was no answer.

He went back to his Ovaro, untied his blanket and carried it back to the corpse. He spread the blanket out on the grass and started the process of rolling the body on it. Something sparkled in the grass. He leaned over and picked it up. A small silver button with a heart stamped on it. Something from a woman's coat. He dropped it into his pocket.

When the blanket was wrapped tight, he hefted the body up on his shoulder and carried it over to the stallion. He slung it across the animal's back and grabbed the rope. A few minutes later the kid was cinched tight and Fargo was swinging up in the saddle.

Two minutes later he was on his way to Cawthorne.

2

Karen Byrnes had no more than opened the door and stepped inside when she saw the frown on Sheriff Tom Cain's face. She knew she was a nuisance and she really didn't give a damn.

A regional newspaper had once called Sheriff Cain "the handsomest lawman in the region." Much as she disliked the man, she had to give him his bearing and looks. Sitting now behind his desk in his usual black suit, white shirt and black string tie, the gray-haired man had the noble appearance of a Roman senator. It was said that he'd always looked this age, fifty or so, even when he was only thirty. It was also said that many gunfighters had mistaken the man's premature gray for a slowing of his abilities. He'd killed well over two dozen men in his time.

The office was orderly: a desk, gun racks on the east wall, WANTED posters on the right. The windows were clean, the brass spittoon gleamed and the wood stacked next to the pot-bellied stove fit precisely into the wooden box. Tom Cain was famous for keeping things neat. People kidded him about it all the time.

The hard blue eyes assessed Karen now. She tried to dismiss their effect on her. Somehow even a glance from Cain made her feel like a stupid child who was wasting his time.

"There's no news, Karen."

"Been two days, Tom."

"I realize it's been two days, Karen."

"They found the other two right away."

"Pure luck. That's how things work out sometimes."

She had planned to let her anger go this time. She would confront him with the fact that if her brother Clete was dead that would make three young men who had been murdered in Cawthorne within the past month. And the legendary town tamer Tom Cain hadn't been able to do a damned thing about it. The father of one of the victims had stood up at a town council meeting and accused Cain of not being up to the task of finding the killer. He had immediately been dragged out of the meeting. In Cawthorne nobody insulted Tom Cain. When he'd come here four years ago nobody had been safe. Two warring gangs of outlaws held the town for ransom. Many of the citizens had started to pack up their things and leave. To the shock and pleasure of everybody, Cain had needed only five months to set the gangs to running. Eleven of them were buried in the local cemetery. It was downright sacrilegious to insult Tom Cain.

"My mother's dying, Tom. You know that. Her heart's bad enough—if we don't find Clete—"

He stood up, straightened his suit coat and came around the desk. Just as he reached her she began to cry, something she'd promised herself she wouldn't do. He gathered her up and took her to him, her pretty face reaching well below his neck. He let her cry and she resented it and appreciated it at the same time.

"We're all just so scared, Tom. Especially my mother."

His massive hand cupped the back of the small blond head and pressed it to him.

"I'm going to find him, Karen. I promise you that. And I'm going to find out who killed the other ones, too. I haven't had any luck yet but I think that's going to change."

She leaned away from him, looked up into the handsome face. "Did you find out something?"

"I don't want to say anything just yet, Karen. I don't want to have bad luck by talking about it."

Despite the situation, she smiled. That was another thing they always said about Tom Cain. Him and his damned superstitions.

"Excuse me," said the slim older deputy Pete Rule, coming through the door that separated the four cells in back from the front office. Rule wore a faded work shirt. A star was pinned to one of the pockets. There was a melancholy about Rule that Karen had always wondered about. Cain's other deputies were basically gunslingers. She wondered why somebody as quiet and often gentle as Rule would have signed on. "Afternoon, Karen."

"Hello, Pete," she said, slipping from Cain's arms. She'd liked Rule ever since she'd seen him jump into a rushing river and pluck out a two-year-old girl who'd wandered into it.

"We'll find him, Karen," Rule said. "That's a promise."

Karen nodded, a bit embarrassed now that she'd been so angry.

"You tell your mother she's in my prayers," Cain said.

"Thanks for helping us. If you weren't here—" She felt tears dampen her eyes again.

"You better go get yourself one of those pieces of apple pie that Mrs. Gunderson's serving over to the café for dinner tonight," Cain said. "She snuck me a slice and I'll tell you I felt better about things right away. And I suspect she'd let you take a piece home for your mother, too."

At the door, she said, "If you hear anything—"

"We'll be at your door ten seconds after we get any kind of word at all."

She nodded to each of them and then left.

"I know one thing," Rule said. "He ain't alive. He's just like them other two."

"Yeah," Cain said, almost bitterly. "And when we find him, I'll be the one who has to tell her."

A little girl in a dress made of feed sacks was the first resident of Cawthorne to see the body of Clete Byrnes. She had just finished shooing her little brother inside for supper when she turned at the sound of a horse and there, passing right by her tiny front yard was a big man on a stallion just now entering the town limits. She knew that there was a man in the blanket tied across the horse because she could see his boots. She wondered if this was Clete Byrnes. Her dad knew Byrnes from the days when he'd worked out at the Bar DD. Byrnes was all her dad talked about at the supper table the past two nights. He said he figured Byrnes was dead but then her mother got mad and shushed him for saying that in front of the four children.

She waved at the big man on the horse and he waved back. Then she ran inside to share her news.

Cawthorne had once been nothing more than a cattle town but these days it was a commercial hub for ranchers and farmers from all around. Fargo started seeing small, inexpensive houses right after he waved to the little girl. He traveled the main road from there into town. At indigo dusk, the stars already fierce, the mountain chill winterlike, he reached the three-block center of Cawthorne. Most of the false-fronted businesses had closed for the day but two cafés and four saloons were noisy as hell and obviously planned to stay that way.

Every few yards somebody on the plank walk would stop to peer at him. There was a fair share of buggy, wagon and horse traffic but somehow, even before they saw the blanket on the back of the Ovaro, they seemed to know that this was the horse everybody in town had been dreading to see.

They had to wait until Fargo came closer to confirm what they suspected. Then they jerked a bit at the sight of the blanket or cursed under their breath or said a prayer.

Fargo watched for a sign identifying the sheriff's office. He had to pass by the saloons before reaching it. A couple of whores stood on the porches of their respective saloons. Fargo had known enough of them in his time—and had liked a hell of a lot of them—to know that these two had stepped out just to get away from the cloying stench and grubbing hands of life inside.

The sheriff's office was at the end of a block that fronted on a riverbank. The building was long, narrow, adobe. As he dismounted and started to tie the reins of his Ovaro to the hitching post, he turned to see shadow-shapes in the gathering darkness. The word was out. Only a few of those in the business district knew about Clete Byrnes as yet but soon most of Cawthorne would. A half-dozen shadow-shapes hurried down the street toward Fargo. The first wave of ghouls.

He walked up to the door and shoved it open. A gaunt man in a faded work shirt and a star came around the desk. "Everything all right?"

Fargo noted that the man's first instinct wasn't to go for his gun. A good sign. Too many gun-happy lawmen around.

"I've got a body out here. His papers said his name is Clete Byrnes."

"Oh, damn, that poor family of his. What happened to him?"

"He was shot three times."

Fargo walked back out on the plank walk. By now twenty people had formed a semicircle around the Ovaro and its lifeless passenger. Men, women, even a pair of towheaded kids who might have been twins. An elderly gentleman with a cane carried a smoky lantern that he held up to the corpse. "Did somebody say it's Clete? I always knew that boy'd end up like this."

"Well, that's a hell of a thing to say," a woman wrapped in a black shawl snapped. "And I'll remember it when we bury you too. I'll have some choice things to say then, myself."

A few of the people laughed, making the scene even stranger.

The deputy shouted, "Now you get away from here and get on about your business."

"We got a right to be here, Pete. Same as you do."

"Is that right, Sam? I guess I can't see your badge because it's so dark. But maybe somebody made you a deputy without me knowing it. We need to sort this thing out."

"Who's the one who brought him in?"

The deputy offered Fargo his hand. "Pete Rule."

"Skye Fargo," the Trailsman said as they shook.

"Hey, I've heard of him!" one of the men said.

"Now, c'mon folks. This whole situation is bad enough. Just please go on about your business."

They left resentfully, calling Rule names as they shuffled away.

Cold moonlight gave Rule enough of a look at the face of the corpse to know who he was seeing. "It's Clete, all right." He shook his head. "Third one in a month."

"Any idea if they're connected?"

"That's what the sheriff is trying to figure out. They were friends, hell-raisers but they never got into any serious trouble. That's what makes this whole thing so damned strange. Who'd want to kill them?"

From down the street came the clatter of a buckboard. All Fargo could see of the man driving it was a top hat. Who the hell would wear a top hat in a town like Cawthorne?

"Here comes Charlie Friese."

"Who's Friese?"

"The undertaker."

"Somebody must've told him about the body."

"He just seems to know. He's got an instinct for it. A lot of folks around here think he's supernatural."

"He wears a top hat?"

"Wait'll you see his cape," Rule laughed.

The buckboard pulled up. Silver steam poured from the nostrils of the horses pulling the vehicle. Rule hadn't been joking about the cape. Fargo still couldn't get a look at the man's face as he stepped down from the buckboard.

"Looks like you've got some business, Charlie. They found the Byrnes boy."

Friese stepped into the light cast from inside the sheriff's office and lifted off his top hat. Shining shoulder-length red hair swung free and a full feminine mouth opened and said, "It's Sarah, Pete. My dad's down with the gout again." Her body was as rich with female promise as her face. Slender but sumptuous at the same time.

"You wearin' your dad's outfit now?"

"People don't take me seriously if I don't. They think I'm

just some nineteen-year-old who doesn't know anything. People are used to Dad's getup. He scares them a little bit. He likes it, too. He's always laughing about it." She touched a hand to the Ovaro's neck. "What a beautiful horse. I'm just sorry he had to bring Clete home. Poor Karen and her mother. They were praying he wouldn't be dead." Her emerald eyes settled on Fargo. "Where did you find him?"

Fargo told her.

"Same as the other two. I wish we knew who was doing this." An ivory hand appeared beneath an edge of the cape. "Sarah Friese."

"You ever heard of the Trailsman?" Rule said.

"Sure."

"Well, that's who you're shaking hands with."

She smiled. "Dad'll be sorry he wasn't here. Are you just passing through, Mr. Fargo?"

"I hope so." Fargo nodded to the buckboard. "Now I imagine we need to get the body on the buckboard."

"I'd appreciate the help."

With Fargo and Rule working together, Clete Byrnes' corpse presented no difficulty. Fargo untied him and they carried him to the back of the buckboard and set him inside.

A larger crowd had gathered. This one remained twenty yards away. One of the onlookers carried a torch. A few lanterns blazed in the gloom.

Before climbing up on the seat again, Sarah Friese said, "I hope I see you before you leave, Mr. Fargo." She wasn't coy. She was straightforward and Fargo liked that. She was interested in his company and he was certainly interested in hers.

"I'd like that, too."

When she was seated and the reins gathered in her hands, she glanced down at Rule. "Sheriff Cain is going to catch a whole lot of hell for this, Pete. My dad said that at church the other night the minister said maybe the sheriff just wasn't up to the job of finding out who killed these boys. That's not the kind of talk you usually hear from a minister. Not our minister, anyway."

"He doesn't like it any better than anybody else does, Sarah. You know that. And besides—" He hesitated. "Well, we're working on something. That's all I'll say for now."

"I have faith in the sheriff, Pete, but a lot of people think he may need to call in some help on this."

She turned the buckboard around expertly and headed back down the street. The crowd parted for her. A few of the drunker ones ran alongside the buckboard trying to get a look at the dead man.

Rule waved Fargo into the office. Fargo started rolling a cigarette for himself.

"Appreciate your help with this. A lot of people would have just left him there."

Fargo shrugged. "Guess I'd appreciate it if somebody'd bring me into town if it was me. Seemed the decent thing to do, is all."

"I reckon that's why you've got such a good reputation, Mr. Fargo."

Fargo smiled. "In some quarters, maybe. But there are plenty of people who'd like to get their guns on me." He scratched a lucifer against the sole of his boot and lighted his cigarette. "No leads on the killer yet?"

"Not yet."

"Lawmen have been known to bring in the Pinkertons."

Rule took a corncob pipe from his shirt pocket and a sack of pipe tobacco from the desk top. "Not this sheriff. He's real independent. Some people like that, some don't. I was a drunk when he found me. Couldn't hold a job. He helped me give up John Barleycorn and become a deputy. So I've got no complaints."

Fargo went to the door. Then remembered something. He took the button from his pocket and carried it back to Rule. "This mean anything to you?"

Rule gave him an odd look. "Lady's button, isn't it?"

"Yeah. Found it near Clete Byrnes' body."

Rule shook his head. "Hmm, never seen anything like it before."

Fargo put the button back in his pocket. "Think I'll find

the livery and then get myself some beer," he said. "You got a decent hotel here?"

"The Royale's good. And pretty cheap. Sheriff'll want to talk to you."

"I won't be hard to find."

Fargo walked out into the chill mountain night, mounted up and eased down the street toward the livery stable.

Welcome to Cawthorne, he thought.

Hearing footsteps behind him, Fargo turned, his hand dropping to his gun. In the dim lamplight of the street, he saw a chunky man in a city suit and derby scurrying after him. Fargo faced him, keeping his hand near his holster. Fargo had just come from the livery stable.

"You want something?"

"Just to talk to you."

"About what?"

"Why about the body, what else?" Then the man doffed his hat and Fargo saw a face that time and alcohol had not treated kindly. "I'm Barney O'Malley. I'm the reporter for the *Cawthorne Clarion*."

Sure as hell not what I want to get into anyway, Fargo thought. Talking to some damned newspaperman who'll just distort what I have to say.

O'Malley, fleshy of body as well as face, whipped out a small notebook from his back pocket and said, "So let me ask you a few questions."

"That's a pretty small notebook. Fits right in your back pocket."

"It's my lucky notebook." He said this without irony.

His lucky notebook, Fargo thought. The thing looked like something a schoolchild would use. Only the black leather cover gave it an adult aspect. And how lucky could it be? This man was obviously a shabby drunkard. He needed a lot more luck than this notebook had given him.

"How about I ask you a few questions?"

"What?"

"Don't you have something better to do than bother me?

11

That's question number one. And question number two is how can you write in the dark like this?"

O'Malley lived up to his Irish name. He blasted Fargo right back, his words carrying the distinctive aroma of cheap whiskey on the night air. "First of all, who the hell else would I bother? You brought Clete Byrnes in, didn't you? And second of all, you're talking to a real reporter, mister. I've worked for papers in Chicago and St. Lou and Denver. I'm no hayseed scribbler."

"And I bet the bottle got you fired from every one of them."

O'Malley, who looked more and more like an overstuffed leprechaun the longer Fargo watched him, came right back. "Alcohol is my heritage. Alcohol is my energy. Alcohol is my truth. And if the editors of this world can't understand that then I feel sorry for them. They're missing out on some of the best journalism being done this side of the Mississippi River."

Despite himself Fargo was amused by the man. He certainly didn't back down. "So what do you want to know?"

"That's more like it."

"I'm glad you approve."

"I'm told your name is Skye Fargo."

"That's correct."

"That would make you the Trailsman."

"That's what they tell me."

"That's pretty big news for a town like Cawthorne. The Trailsman stopping by."

"I thought you wanted to talk about me bringing in Clete Byrnes."

"Just so. But you'll be a big part of the story. Almost as big as the body itself."

Referring to Byrnes as "the body" would have offended Fargo if he hadn't been used to the objective—some would say callous—way reporters went about their jobs. The story was all-important. The people involved were just stage props.

Fargo said, "You ready? Here's what happened. Then I want you to get the hell away from me."

"Fair enough. Give me the story."

Fargo rolled himself a smoke as he laid out the circumstances in which he'd found Clete Byrnes. He even took the silver button from his shirt pocket and showed it to O'Malley. The journalist held it between thumb and forefinger and rolled it around and held it up to the light. "Don't think Helen'd have anything as fancy as this."

"Who's Helen?"

"Crotchety old widow who lives on the land where you found Byrnes." O'Malley shrugged. "Last year somebody broke into a local woman's house and stole some things. But I don't know that that'd have anything to do with this. It's sure Byrnes didn't have it on him. So what I want to know now is what the Trailsman plans to do next?"

"The name's Fargo."

"The Trailsman's a lot more dramatic."

Fargo laughed. "I can see why they'd get rid of you even if you didn't have a problem with the bottle."

"They 'got rid of me' as you say because they didn't like me showing them up for the amateurs they were." The derby on his head once more, he leaned a few inches closer and said, "Just as I'm doing here in Cawthorne. The owner here is a man named Amos Parrish. He's never worked on a large newspaper in his life. But he's under the mistaken impression that he's doing me some kind of favor by paying me slave wages for work he could never do himself. He's even taken to putting both our names on the pieces I write, claiming that people will believe it more readily if we've both signed it. He's jealous, of course. And he'll be even more jealous when I crack this case."

"The killings?"

"Indeed, the killings."

"Do you actually know something or are you just talking?"

O'Malley leaned back and bestowed an impish grin on Fargo. A leprechaun for sure. "So you're intrigued, Fargo."

"I'm intrigued if you know something that's a fact."

O'Malley touched his chest as if he'd been mortally

13

wounded. "And what do you think I deal in, sir, except facts? The truth, as I said, is to be found in the bottle. The bottle tells me many things and it never lies."

Fargo's amusement was wearing thin. "If you know something, you should tell Sheriff Cain."

O'Malley barked a laugh. "Cain? You trust Tom Cain?"

"He's the sheriff."

"He's a town tamer. There's a difference. An honest sheriff does what's best for the town. A town tamer does what's best for him."

"Well, if you won't tell him how about telling me?"

"Sir, do you have any idea how a reporter works?"

Fargo yawned. "No, but I'm afraid I'm about to find out."

"A reporter works in secrets and he keeps his secrets. If I were to reveal what I'm working on right now this town would explode. So I"—he doffed his derby once again—"I keep it under my hat as they say. My derby to be exact. You'll be the man I turn to—if you promise me that you won't share my secrets with Cain."

Fargo wasn't sure what to make of the Irish drunk. He was a windbag, that was for certain. And a damned irritating one at some points. But maybe his experiences on big-city newspapers—if they weren't just a figment of his besotted imagination—might actually make him the one man in town who could sort through everything that had happened and make sense of it.

"It's not always safe to keep secrets. If you're on to somebody he may be on to you."

"I keep a derringer up my sleeve. Spent some time on riverboats as a gambler."

"The killer's going to come at you with a hell of a lot more than a derringer if he thinks you can identify him."

"That, Mr. Fargo, is my concern, not yours."

And with that he once again doffed his hat and disappeared into the night.

3

Trail dust and a good night's sleep were Fargo's two main concerns when he checked into the Royale. The nattily attired desk clerk assured him that both Fargo's desires could be taken care of with no problem. With a great deal of pleasure, in fact, he said in his best desk clerk voice.

The lobby was filled with drummers. The checkered suits and the black bags gave them away. Fargo enjoyed his travels. He was just glad he didn't have to wear stupid suits and hawk worthless products to naïve men and women across the West. And not all of them were harmless. He'd run into a few snake oil salesmen who peddled everything from opium to murder. He'd once shot a drummer who hired out as a killer when he visited a town. He usually managed to escape in time. Until he happened to be in the same town as Fargo at the same time.

The room was small but clean and the mattress seemed to be new. He sat down to test it and liked what he felt. Now for the trail dust. The desk clerk had told him to go to room D where he would find a big aluminum tub. He would see that a woman was there to assist Fargo. Fargo brought clean clothes and found room D. The woman proved to be a fine piece of goods, dark—probably Italian—with sensuously sculpted features and a blue cotton dress that revealed rich breasts and hips made for handling.

Near the big tub were four buckets of water. Steam rose from them. And on a table behind the buckets were towels and soap.

"My name is Antonia."

"Skye Fargo."

"You're a big one."

"And you're a pretty one."

She obviously enjoyed the compliment. He pulled the silver button from his pocket and showed it to her. "You ever see this before?"

"No. It is from a woman's garment."

"That's what I figured."

"Where did you find it?"

He changed the subject. "How about that bath?"

"I will step out while you take your clothes off. There is soapy water in the tub. It is cool. I'll use the other buckets to heat it up as we go along."

In a graceful glide she left the room. Fargo stripped down, piled his dusty clothes in a heap, then lowered himself carefully into the tub. The water was more than cool, it was downright cold. A couple of shudders and he was fine. "C'mon back."

Antonia appeared and silently went to one of the buckets. She took the handle with long fingers and carried it to the tub. "I will pour slowly. You tell me when it's too hot."

As she bent over to pour the water, he noticed how her full breasts pressed against the blue cotton of her dress. He also noticed that she noticed his gaze. She smiled.

He leaned back, muscular arms on the sides of the tub, closed his eyes. This was a pleasure a wandering man like himself didn't experience all that often. He might as well enjoy it.

She even began to sing, which relaxed him all the more. She had a sweet voice. Too bad he couldn't understand the Italian lyrics.

"What's the song about?"

"Two lonely people who meet on a street in Rome one summer night."

"Do they stay lonely?"

Her laugh was as sweet as her singing voice. "Not for long. That's what the song is really about. How they meet and come together."

"I think I like that song."

"It's one of my favorites, too."

"Does the desk clerk know you favor certain guests?"

"Very few guests," she said sadly, "for very few appeal to me. And anyway, he is sleeping with the owner's wife. I keep his secrets and he keeps mine."

"That's a decent arrangement."

"But he sees her many times more than I choose to favor guests with my body."

"Maybe you're too choosy."

"I've thought of that. But it's like that song I sing. How two people meet and come together. They must be the right people. Now let me pour more water in the tub."

"I can't figure out if you're trying to scald me or drown me."

"You will see what I am trying to do in very short order."

Ten minutes and a bucket and a half later, Fargo found himself sinking into sleep. The song had become a kind of lullaby and the hot water was making him want to doze off. But he was surprised to find that she had a very satisfying way of getting his attention again.

She had slid her hand under the sudsy top of the water and taken hold of his manhood. Her mere touch had brought him to full alert.

"You are as big as I had hoped."

Fargo laughed. "You like them big?"

"I am an Italian girl. We are a sensual country. We take our pleasure seriously. Why not have a lover who can fill you up and make you gasp?"

Her words were making his lance even stiffer. The blinding tension leading up to lovemaking was on him. His breath came in short animallike gasps. But he knew there was no way he could fit her into this small tub.

Her mouth found his, her tongue driving him up from the tub, dripping soapy water as he rose. But she arched herself away from him as her tongue flicked through his entire mouth, making him even harder. "It wouldn't be right to get my dress wet. Let me spread towels out for us. And then I will undress."

Fargo stepped out of the tub, his spear leading the way. Watching her undress only made his lust more urgent. She was a ripe woman with beautifully turned breasts and sumptuous curves. The curly hair at the top of her legs was as dark as her flashing eyes. He watched her bend over spreading the towels and could no longer hold himself. He eased up behind her and pressed himself against her. His entire body lurched as she gasped, "Oh, God!" Her breasts spilled over his hands. He held them tight and then began playing with one of them between his thumb and forefinger. She began insinuating herself against his manhood with greater passion than before.

They sank to the towels slowly, her turning in his arms as they did so. When he knelt between her he spread her legs and eased down to part her thighs and bring his mouth to her. When his tongue tasted her she writhed upward with her hips and then grabbed his hair with such ferocity it was a wonder she didn't tear some of it out by the roots.

He kept her dancing on the tip of his tongue until she screamed with enough savagery to be heard by everybody on the floor. In the last stages of thrashing wet joy she said, "Now, now be in me!"

Fargo didn't need more of an invitation than that. He drew himself up and let her guide him in.

"You are so big!" she cried.

He put himself in very deep and then began to twist and wriggle out a furious rhythm they were both comfortable with. He'd been right about those hips. He used them to steer their passion, slipping his hands now and then to her ample buttocks to slam himself deeper and deeper into her. After a time he varied his strokes, short stabs, long lances, almost teasing her. Her legs were over his shoulders now and she brought them together as a vise behind his neck.

When they were both working their way toward mutual frenzy, he eased himself out of her and then turned her over. She positioned herself on her palms and knees as he drove himself inside her. Once again he used her hips as a way of steering the sex and she was happy to let him drive their mutual satisfaction.

By the time he finished, he'd given up counting the number of her explosions. It had to be more than ten.

Her eyes shone like stars as she lay there looking up at him. He was on his haunches now, grabbing his makings from his clothes.

"I will never forget this."

"Neither will I," he said. A harmless lie.

"You know what is funny?"

"What is funny?"

"The way you sweat. You know what must happen now, don't you?"

"No, I guess I don't."

"I will have to give you another bath. The water will be cooler now. But I am sure you will be much more relaxed this time."

"You may have something there, you know that?"

She stood up. She was lacquered with sweat, too. She grabbed one of the towels from the floor and began drying herself. "Antonia will sleep well tonight. I am sure of it." She pointed to the tub. "Now my well-hung friend, sit in the water again and I will wash the hair and the body the way I should have. But I was too distracted with my own lust to do a good job."

"You didn't hear me complaining, did you?"

"Nor I," she said. "You did not hear Antonia complaining either, did you?"

Fargo pushed through the batwings of the Gold Mine ready for some whiskey now that he'd had a romp with the accommodating woman who worked for the hotel.

At this time of night, a saloon like this one should have been crowded with men wanting to get drunk and have a good time with cards, tall tales and a few of the soiled doves who prowled the large smoky room.

Tonight though, harsh voices told of tension and anger.

19

The three girls in their low-cut blue taffeta dresses sat at a table talking to one another. Apparently none of the customers were much interested in them right now. The discovery of Clete Byrnes had put a pall on any fun.

Fargo strode to the long bar, found an empty space and asked for a shot of whiskey and a schooner of beer. The bartender was a fat man in a dirty white shirt and red sleeve garters. He kept right on talking to another customer, his only recognition of Fargo's request a curt nod. Then he stopped talking to the other man and stared at Fargo.

"You're the fella that found Clete, ain't ya?"

"Guess I am."

"The Trailsman."

"That's what some folks call me. Just as soon be called by my real name."

There was so much conversation that only the men at the bar heard the exchange between Fargo and the bartender. They all angled around so they could see the man who'd found the Byrnes boy. One of them shouted to a table of drinkers, "Here's the man who found Clete!"

So much for having a few peaceful, solitary drinks. Fargo never liked the limelight. Being the center of attention often meant trouble of one kind or another, especially in a saloon full of drunken, sullen men.

Even the girls in the taffeta dresses quit talking to take a look at the rangy man standing at the bar.

"This here's the Trailsman," the bartender shouted. And pointed at Fargo.

Muttered words. Some had heard of the Trailsman, some hadn't. But right now he was the most interesting part of this terrible night.

"You did us a favor, mister," said a man in a business suit and a long, fancy mustache. "At least we don't have to wonder if Clete's alive anymore."

"Just doing what anybody else would."

"You give that man anything he wants, Jeff," said another man, this one brawny. He also looked like a businessman. "I'll be paying for it."

"Nice of you, friend. But not necessary."

"My pleasure."

One of the girls stood up and made her way over to Fargo. Ordinarily she'd try to get him to buy some watered-down whiskey and then woo him to one of the tiny rooms on the second floor. But the sadness in the brown eyes told Fargo that the girl had been affected by Byrnes' death. "He was a friend of mine."

"A lot of people seemed to like him."

"The way he treated us girls, a real gentleman. That's hard to come by in a place like this." She touched Fargo's arm. "Just wanted you to know that the three of us appreciate you bringing him in. It's better to know than not know."

Her lower lip began trembling. She ducked her head, turned and hurried back to her table where the other two girls stood up to take her in their arms.

"Here's the bottle," the bartender said behind Fargo's back. "On the house."

Just as Fargo started to wheel around and pour himself a drink, some kind of explosive scene developed at one of the tables near the back of the place. Fargo watched as a lean blond man in a blue shirt and Levi's shook off the hands of his friends and started stalking toward the bar.

"You're just drunk, Kenny. And he's nobody to mess with!" This came from one of the men who'd tried to grab on to Kenny and stop him.

"Sit down, Kenny, you dumb bastard!" a man at a table near the front shouted. "We got enough problems tonight!"

"You shut your face, Stevens," Kenny snapped, "or I'll take care of you before I get to Fargo here."

The bartender joined in. "You just keep right on walkin' out those batwings, Kenny. You been barred from here before and if you start any trouble here tonight, I'll bar you for good."

"How do we know this one here didn't kill Clete?" Kenny said. "And there's only one way to find out."

"You didn't hear who he is?" the bartender said. "This here's the Trailsman."

"You think I'm scared of somebody with a pumped-up name? Especially when he killed poor Clete?"

Fargo moved away from the bar. "No call to make this any worse a night than it already is. I didn't kill your friend. And I don't want to have to kill you, either."

"You talk big."

Kenny was faster than Fargo expected. The man's right hand dropped to his holster, the .45 started gleaming in the light of the Rochester lamps and—

And in a single swift move, Fargo spun back toward the bar, grabbed the whiskey bottle by the neck and hurled it at the other man's gun hand. The bottle smashed so hard against Kenny's hand that his shot went wild as he squeezed it off. He stood there looking confused and angry, as if some diabolical magician's trick had just been played on him.

Then he made a move so dumb Fargo gave up coddling him. Drunk as he was, Kenny dove in the direction of the .45 that had been knocked from his hand and then skidded a few feet away.

Fargo had put two bullets in Kenny's gun hand before the man was even close enough to his weapon to retrieve it.

Kenny had a good pair of lungs. He cried out with enough force to break every single glass behind the bar. He sank to his knees cursing and wailing. Nobody moved to help or comfort him. He'd been a damned fool and this was no night for damned fools.

"I saw you do the same thing down in Waco one time."

The voice was familiar. Fargo turned to glance at the batwing doors. Towering above them was an imposing man with a wind-leathered face and a pair of eyes so ice blue they were almost silver. The silver hair complemented the eyes.

"Well, I'll be damned," Fargo laughed.

The batwings parted and the outsize man stepped into the saloon. Smiling and imposing himself on the situation. "That's right, Fargo, Skye. It's Tom Cain. And you sure will be damned. You'll be burning in the lowest, hottest part of hell as I remember."

Steve Trotter the town tamer now carried the name Tom Cain? Why?

But Cain didn't give Fargo much time to think about it. He cleared the distance between them in four long steps and shoved forth a hand big enough to make even Fargo's seem small.

He winked at Fargo and said, "Kenny here's part of the welcoming committee."

"I kind of gathered that."

As soon as they were done shaking hands, Cain looked at the men nearest the crouching Kenny and said, "Get his ass out of here before I throw him in jail for a couple of weeks just for the hell of it."

Then, to the bartender, "It's a shame Fargo here had to waste that liquor bottle on Kenny. How about another one? Fargo and I have got some catchin' up to do."

Once they were sitting down, Steve Trotter said, "Had a little trouble back there down the trail, so I thought it might help things along if I changed my name."

"So you're not Steve Trotter anymore?"

"Well, I guess I never did get around to tellin' you, Fargo. Steve Trotter wasn't actually my name either."

Fargo had always known that Cain was a shady actor. In the days when Fargo had known him he was a town tamer who, after setting the town to rights, made sure that he left town with plenty of money and the affection of ladies young and old, married or not. He was a scoundrel and Fargo should have disliked him. But the man had such incredible gall that all a person could do was stand back and be amazed at how many different roles he could play when he needed to. He could be the sober, fatherlike lawman; the mean, trigger-happy gunny; the slicker who could talk a duchess into bed. He was like one of those animals who could adapt their coloration to whatever the situation was.

The men in the Gold Mine had returned to their drinking and their cards and their cheap feeling of the girls. Fargo and Cain sat at a table in the back away from the others.

"On your way to Denver, then?"

"Yeah. See a couple of people there."

"I may be movin' on. Probably time I do. But before I do"—he raised his glass of bourbon—"thanks for bringing the kid in. That's the only thing that's keeping me here now. I want to find out who's behind all these killings. Go out with people respecting me for doing my job. If I leave before that—"

"Town this size, I imagine people are spooked."

"Spooked and for the first time since I cleaned this place up, they've got their doubts about me. They're starting to wonder if maybe I'm all right with a gun but not so good when it comes to figuring out murders. I'm not used to that kind of treatment and I don't like it." He leaned back in his chair and said, "I even thought of calling in the Pinkertons for some help."

Fargo remembered what Deputy Pete Rule had said. That Cain wouldn't ever call in the Pinkertons. Apparently Cain didn't share his thoughts with his underlings.

"Say, don't I remember you working with the Pinkertons a few times?"

"A few times I helped a couple of them out." Fargo smiled. "I wouldn't want to make a habit of it, though."

"Well, how about helping me?"

"Helping you how?"

"Doing it the way the Pinkertons would. How they find killers."

"You probably know a lot more about that than I do."

"Hell, no, Skye. I tame towns. That means I use my fists and my gun. Not my brain. Besides, we'd make a good team."

Fargo shook his head. "I'm not a detective and I'm leaving town tomorrow morning."

"I'm in a bind here, Skye."

"Well, you've been in binds before and you sure seem to have done all right."

"If I could take you to the town council with me—tell them you're helping me with this—"

"Who's your friend, Sheriff?"

Fargo glanced up to see a pretty but worn dance hall girl with her dark hair pinned up around a blue ribbon. A deep-cut neckline revealed delectable full breasts. She was older than the others and in a few years would be too wasted to compete with the new girls. But for now she was vivacious despite her fading looks.

"Mame, this is my old friend Skye Fargo. They call him the Trailsman."

"I like the company you keep, Sheriff." Mame's blue eyes traced Fargo's face, obviously liking what she saw. "Handsome man."

"Hey, I thought you said I was the handsome man." Cain winked at Fargo.

"Well, I'd say you have some competition."

"I may just throw you in jail, Mame."

"Long as you put me in the same cell as Mr. Fargo here."

"How about this, Mame?" Cain said, taking her hand. "If you want to get to know Skye better then you have to help me convince him to stick around and help me find who's been killing these boys."

The playfulness left Mame's voice. "I feel so sorry for Karen and her mother. Not everybody in my line of work gets treated well. But the Byrneses have been nice to me since the day I got here."

"Then while I go get us some more drinks, you sit here and convince Fargo to stay."

Mame took Cain's place. Fargo liked her face the more he studied it. Intelligence and caring there. She probably had the same story most soiled doves did, running away from a bad family somewhere on the plains of the Midwest and ending up whoring because she couldn't figure out anything else to do. The trouble was, a man could only hear that same story so many times without being cynical. Must have been something else some of these girls could've done besides lying down for very little money. But he'd taken to Mame, no doubt about it.

"I knew all three of those boys." She smiled. "And you

can take 'know' any way you want. I'm a businesswoman. I run the girls here and I want to make a profit for the saloon and myself as well."

"Any idea what's behind somebody killing them?"

"Not specifically. But a while back they started acting nervous."

"All three of them?"

"Yes. Especially Clete. He wasn't as tough as the other two anyway. I could always read his face. If he was unhappy about something, I could tell. Same with when he was worried. And lately he'd been worried."

"How about the other two?"

"They didn't strike me as worried exactly. But they started getting into fights here. They were usually pretty easygoing. But something had riled them up and they stayed riled up right up to the time they got killed." A long slender hand eased across the table and covered Fargo's. "Tom must have a lot of faith in you. I don't ever recall him admitting that he needed help. That surprised me. And that means that he thinks you might know how to solve this. And believe me, this town needs it solved. Everybody's scared."

"Like I told him, Mame, I'm not a detective."

"You're probably more of a detective than Tom is. He thinks with his fists."

"So do I pretty much."

"I've made a study of men's eyes, Mr. Fargo. I can pretty well size them up just by watching how they react to things. I know your reputation as a fighter and a gunman but you're also intelligent. You can work through things. And that's what we need now. The men who come in here and get beered up are a pretty good cross section of town. People are getting worked up. They're starting to look at their neighbors, wondering if they might have something to do with it. I've seen it happen in towns before like this. It can get pretty ugly."

Cain was back with two schooners of beer and a shot of bourbon for the lady. "Well, I'll bet you've convinced him to stay on for a while. You never miss."

"I told him you weren't smart enough to figure this out on your own." She smiled. "Sorry. But that's the truth, Tom."

"My biggest admirer. Or couldn't you tell that, Skye?"

Skye smiled. He imagined that Tom and Mame had spent many a night together and that they'd become skilled hands at joshing each other this way. One of the other girls appeared and bent down and whispered something to Mame. The woman stood up. "Need to take care of a little business. I hope I see you again, Skye. I think we could get to be good friends."

After she'd gone, Cain said, "That woman knows more about sex than even I do." Then: "So did she convince you?"

"Afraid not, Tom." Fargo stood up. Yawned. Stretched. "I'm turning in, Steve—Tom. Need to get up early. And I won't be seeing you again."

"That town council's after me, Skye. I really need—"

"Won't do any good, Tom. I'm leaving town."

"I could give you some money, Skye—"

"I told you. I want to go see my friends. That's more important to me than money. So, so long, Tom. I'm sorry but that's the way it's going to be."

He left the lawman sitting there lifting his drink to his scowling face.

4

In the morning, Fargo shaved, washed up, dressed and packed his saddlebags. At the window of his room he stood smoking a cigarette and looking at the magnificent snow-peaked mountains. Dawn was streaks of soft red and yellow in the sky, staining the mist in the mountains the same colors. It would be a good day to travel and he was eager to get out of town.

In the lobby he noticed three young women sitting on a long couch. They watched him with obvious interest. He tipped his hat to them as he walked out the door. One of them was somebody he might like to spend time with under other circumstances.

The main street was just starting to come alive. Vehicle traffic was light but he could see laborers huddled into heavy jackets making their way to work sites. They had to start early these days because dusk came early.

He'd slept well and felt strong. He decided to eat a solid breakfast before heading for the livery. The food would hold him till nightfall when he had to make camp.

The interior of the café was lost in the smoke of cigarettes, pipes, cigars and the grease it took to prepare too many breakfasts in too little space. Fargo decided to fight smoke with smoke as he waited for his steak and eggs and potatoes. He sat at a wobbly table in back that had just been vacated and lighted his cigarette. At least the smoke was his own.

When he finished his food, he stood up, patted his stomach, slid on his hat and walked outside—right into the three young women he'd seen in the hotel lobby.

"We'd like to talk to you, if we may, Mr. Fargo. My name's Denise Haller. My younger brother was one of the boys who was murdered recently." Denise was full-bodied with auburn hair. "And this is Rebecca Nolan. Her brother was killed, too." Rebecca was a buxom brunette. "And this is Karen Byrnes. You brought her brother's body in yesterday." She was a blue-eyed blond young woman more handsome than pretty.

"I'll tell you, I'm trying to get out of town here as soon as I can. But I guess I can spend a few minutes."

"We'd like to hire you."

"Hire me? For what?"

"To find out who killed our brothers," Karen Byrnes said.

"We met with Sheriff Cain last night. He said that he didn't have any new ideas right now," Denise Haller said. "That's what he's been saying all along."

"And he told us about you," Rebecca Nolan said, dawning sunlight glinting off her dark hair. "He said he tried to convince you to stay but you wouldn't do it. He said that maybe you'd stay if we asked you ourselves. Then Denise thought of trying to hire you. People hire detectives. So we pooled our money." She dug into the pocket of her Levi's. Her yellow shirt and black vest gave her a competent look.

Denise Haller said, "I wanted the three of us to go to your hotel room last night. But Karen said it wouldn't be proper."

"Our brothers are dead and she's worried about propriety," Rebecca Nolan sniffed.

"Well, somebody has to worry about propriety." Karen Byrnes hadn't taken the criticism well.

Fargo held up his hand. "Hold on there. I kind of figured that Cain was probably behind this and I guess I figured right."

"I damned well resent that," Denise Haller snapped. "Our brothers are dead. We didn't need any push to look for help if Sheriff Cain couldn't come up with anything."

"You didn't have to swear," Karen Byrnes said.

"You should've been a nun, Karen," Rebecca Nolan said.

Fargo, despite the situation, laughed. "Ladies, first of all, I'm headed to the livery and then me and my horse are heading out. Second of all, bickering among yourselves is just going to make things worse for everybody, especially you three. And I'm sure that if you give Tom Cain more time—"

"He's too old," Denise Haller said. "And he doesn't have any experience with things like this."

"And he admits it himself," Karen Byrnes said. "He said that right to our faces last night in his office."

The one thing Fargo feared most of all happened just as he looked longingly down the plank walk to the livery and his Ovaro. Rebecca Nolan began crying. Sobbing, really. Burying her face in her hands. Her entire body shook. A woman's tears could cow him faster than bullets.

Just as her friends reached over to hold her, three rough-hewn laborers came out of the café and glanced from the women to Fargo.

"What the hell'd you do to her?" one of the men snarled at Fargo. "You got her all cryin'."

"He was awful to us," Karen Byrnes said. "We asked him for a little assistance and he refused to help us."

One of the other men made a clucking sound. "Out here, mister, a lady asks for help, a man is expected to give it."

"Thank you, sir," Denise Haller said. "It's nice to know that there are at least a few gentlemen in this town."

"Big, strong fella like you," the third man said. "What the hell's wrong with you?"

Denise Haller took her hands from her face. Her cheeks gleamed with tears, But her eyes gleamed with amusement. "He's just a terrible, heartless man, is all."

"Now are you gonna help these ladies or not, mister?"

By now Fargo could see that all three of them were trying to hide their amusement. They'd figured out his allergy to tears and had used it skillfully.

"All right, dammit," Fargo said, resentful that he'd been snookered. "I'll help you."

"Now that's more like it," the second man said. Then to his companions, "We'd better get to work."

Before Fargo left the women, he made them all examine the silver button carefully. None of them recognized it.

In the morning light Sheriff Tom Cain looked much older than he had the night before in the Gold Mine saloon. Severe lines were etched into the corners of his eyes and around his mouth. Liver spots dotted the tops of his hands. And the coffee cup he held in his grip trembled slightly.

Fargo saw all this as he crossed the threshold of the sheriff's office.

Cain raised his cup in salute. "Glad to see you stopped by before you left town."

"I gave it a try but those women you sicced on me convinced me otherwise."

"Sicced on you?" The broad smile. "Now that's an awfully cynical attitude. I simply pointed out that you were the most capable man in this valley to help me out."

"The crying worked pretty well."

Cain set his cup down and poured one for Fargo. "I've found that a woman's tears can be as effective as a bullet sometimes."

"I'll give you twenty-four hours."

"You think you can find the killer that soon?"

"I'm riding out in twenty-four hours, Tom. One way or the other."

Cain handed Fargo the coffee and went over to sit behind his desk. Fargo took the chair under the glass gun case.

"Three killings in less than a month. I'm pretty sure those three were involved in a stagecoach robbery we had about five weeks ago. Fifty thousand dollars was taken. The stagecoach driver and one of the passengers, an Englishman, were killed."

"So who's responsible for killing the boys?"

"I figure somebody else planned the robbery and then decided to get rid of the boys so they couldn't turn on him."

"Any names come to mind?"

"I'd start with the people at the stage line."

"You think the robbers and somebody in the stage company were involved?"

"It's not exactly unheard of, Skye. But there's something else. The stage was carrying the fifty thousand in a strongbox headed for the mines up in the mountains. There'd been a few robberies before and the bank wanted this run to be secret. Well, I don't have to tell you what secret means, do I? Five, six people knew what was on that stage."

"What about the bank? Somebody there knew about it, too."

Cain smiled. "See, you're doing it already."

"Doing what?"

"Acting like a Pinkerton. But no, the bank president is a friend of mine. He swears up and down nobody at the bank would have thrown in with bank robbers. He claims he hires a better class of people." He snorted. "I'm not sure there is any such thing."

"What're the names of the men at the stage company?"

"Kenny and Sam Raines are drivers for the stage line. Kenny's the one you had the run-in with last night. They're still around. I talked to them myself a couple of times but got nowhere. And there's another man who has to be considered. Bob Thomas. He worked there until he was fired two months ago. They claim he was caught stealing from the till. Thomas denies it. He was in pretty good with those three boys. You can't rule him out either."

Cain paused for a sip of coffee. "And there's another man there, the manager, who's deviled me since I came here."

"Deviled you how?"

A laugh. "Why how else have I ever been deviled, Skye? A woman of course. A very beautiful widow named Amy Peters. I actually fell in love with her the first time I saw her."

Fargo rolled his eyes. "You? Fall in love? You've slept with half the women in the West and it never came to that before. That must mean that you've never been able to get her in your bed. And since you can't have her you think you love her."

"Might be some sense to that, Skye. But anyway, there's bad blood between her man Ned Lenihan and me. I—I wasn't always what you might call decent to him when I went after his lady. And I went too far. She hates me as much as he does."

"Why do you think Lenihan is involved?"

"Well, since Lenihan is the manager at the stage company, he's a suspect in the robbery. Lenihan himself was the one who put the money on the stagecoach. And he's got a need for money. He's got a little farm that him and his son have had bad luck on. The bank is calling the note in on it. More coffee?"

Fargo shook his head. Cain got up and went to the stove and poured himself another cup.

Fargo's lake blue eyes narrowed. "What the hell's going on here, Steve, Tom or whatever the hell your name is?"

"Nothing's going on here. I'm asking you for help."

"You don't ask people for help. You're too arrogant."

Cain shrugged. "Used to be too arrogant. Not anymore. Not in this town anyway. Town tamers have a limited number of years when they're in favor. They make a lot of enemies and sometimes those enemies come into some power and start pushing for new blood to wear the star. That's happening here."

"They're forcing you out?" Fargo saw that the trembling had stopped in Cain's hand. Had Cain been faking it for sympathy? Fargo wouldn't put it past him. The man was an actor.

"The town council isn't meeting this morning because they have any faith in me. I've got one friend there and he tells me they're going to force me to call in the Pinks. I'd rather work with you. And that's what I'm going to tell them. You're here right now. It'll take a few days to get a Pink operative here. That'd be my argument."

"Even though I don't know more about detective work than you do?"

The irritating arrogant laugh. "That may be true, Skye. But they don't know that and after I get done pumping up your credentials they'll think you're Pinkerton himself." Seeing that Fargo was going to balk, he held up his hand. The trembling was completely gone. "Most people know your reputation. They'll help you. And you do actually know how the Pinks operate."

"Somewhat."

"Somewhat is good enough for me, Skye. I have no doubt you'll find the killer. And then you know what? I can leave this town. I don't want to leave it with this hanging over me. I've still got one or two more towns left in me. Three unsolved murders wouldn't look good."

"What happened to your hand?"

"My hand?"

"It was shaking like hell when I came in."

"Oh, this?" He held up his hand and after a moment made it start shaking. "Pretty good, huh? I needed to look a little helpless." The laugh again. "It's just in my nature, Skye. Guess I'm a frustrated thespian."

"You're a frustrated something all right," Fargo said, resenting that he'd allowed himself to be trapped into this. Hell, he wanted to be on his way to Denver. And he never wanted to see Tom Cain or whatever he was calling himself ever again.

Fargo could still see the shape of Clete Byrnes' body where it had lain in the grass next to the tree. He hadn't taken the time yesterday to really scout the place the way the Pinkertons usually did. Now he was combing the area for signs of anything that might indicate who had killed him. His Pinkerton friends had told him that if you looked over a crime area carefully you'd be surprised what you'd find. And the silver button had proved the Pinkertons correct. But where did the button come from? What did it have to do with the death of young Byrnes? Or did it have anything to do with it at all?

There were traces of blood in the grass leading from a narrow dusty trail to the beginning of the front yard of the soddie he had seen yesterday. So: shot in the road, dragged to the tree. The person who lived there might have seen something if she'd been in the yard.

The soddie he approached had been upgraded from the usual soddie you found on the frontier. A shingle roof had been built to save the place from leaking rain for one thing and an actual wooden door had been installed. No doubt the place was still home to vermin of every kind—not to mention snakes—but at least the top wouldn't collapse every time the weather turned bad.

A dozen chickens ran frantically around to the left of the place and a wolfhound stood alert watching him. A good time to stop. Fargo made sure his hand was nowhere near his Colt. He raised his voice and spoke to the closed door. "My name's Fargo. I'm working with Sheriff Cain. I'd like to talk to you."

Yesterday he'd walked up to the door. But the wolfhound hadn't been here. And today he sensed that somebody was inside.

"I'll have to keep coming back unless you come out and talk to me. You could save both of us a lot of trouble."

At first the only sound was the wind soughing through the huge pines nearby. He took two steps forward. Another sound—the wolfhound growling, the mouth opening to reveal gleaming white teeth.

The door opened and a tiny woman who was probably in her sixties came out toting a Winchester that was aimed right at Fargo's chest. She wore a flat-crowned black hat, a buckskin shirt, black butternuts and buckskin boots that came up to her knees. She might have been pretty once but years out here had scrubbed most of the prettiness away. She had hard, harsh green eyes. She might have weighed one hundred on a good day.

"Morning, ma'am."

"Don't start none of that 'morning, ma'am' bilge with me. My name's Helen Hardesty and I ain't no ma'am."

"I'm working with Sheriff—"

"What the hell you think I got here? Brick walls? In case you didn't notice, this is a soddie. Meaning I can hear everything you said. And don't try and make me cooperate because you're working with that show-off sheriff. He's nothing to me."

One hundred pounds of pure prairie grit, Fargo thought.

"I found a dead man here yesterday."

"Good for you. I don't know anything about it."

"He was laying right back there. He was probably shot on the trail and dragged by that tree." Fargo turned and pointed. "Seems like you might've heard or seen something."

"Guess you didn't hear me, mister. I don't know anything about it." She waggled the Winchester at him. The wolfhound growled. "You simmer, Samson. I can handle this tinhorn."

Fargo thought, you had to like her. The Eastern papers always talked about "the pioneer spirit" and this was surely it. A slight woman defending herself from a stranger at gunpoint. It was too bad she was lying. She needed some real practice when she decided not to tell the truth.

"Is your husband around?"

"Yep. Back of the soddie. I buried him there three years ago."

"You like living alone?"

"What the hell're these questions about? I already told you I don't know nothing about no killing and I mean exactly what I say."

Maybe if she could look at him when she lied he'd be more likely to believe her. Also, the way she kept gnawing on her lower lip when it was his turn to talk told him that she was nervous about something. He also suspected—brazen as she was with him—that she might be afraid. She put on a hell of a good show. But what if she'd seen the killer and he'd threatened her?

"I'd like to help you, Helen."

"You would, huh? Then you git on that horse of yours and ride out. That'd help me a lot."

"I think you're afraid. I think you saw something and somebody threatened you."

She lost her grit just for a moment. "Who told you that?" But the tone was plaintive. Then: "It's a lie. I didn't see nothing and nobody threatened me, either."

"Whoever threatened you, he's killed one man, maybe more. And maybe he'll decide to kill you."

"I'm tough. I've got this." The barrel of the Winchester gleamed in the sun. "And I've got Samson. Show him, Samson."

The wolfhound stood up abruptly and growled. On cue. As in a circus act.

"I know you're tough. I'll bet you're tough enough to tell the truth."

"And tough enough to get you off my property. Go, Samson!"

The wolfhound leapt directly at Fargo. Teeth bared. Growl deep in its chest and belly. It landed just a few feet in front of Fargo and went into attack formation. But then it stopped.

Fargo felt sweat slick his face. He couldn't think of a single man he was afraid of. He could think of a whole list of animals who gave him nightmares.

Helen Hardesty cackled. "That's my warning shot. You should see your face, mister. You don't look so strong now. I taught Samson to leap like that but then stop short. Scares the hell out of intruders. The next time I give him an order, though, he don't stop short. He goes right for your throat."

"You've got it all figured out."

"I sure do."

"Except for the killer. You're worried he'll come back on you and you don't know what to do about it."

"We're done here, mister. Now I'm goin' back inside and Samson's gonna sit right where he is. I give him the order, he'll tear you apart. You understand?"

She was true to her word. She did an about-face and stalked back to her soddie. Samson stayed in place.

She was right, Fargo thought. They were done here.

Less than a minute later he was in his saddle and headed out.

5

Karen Byrnes came home to the small frame house on the edge of the creek and put herself to work. Her mother had not been able to sleep all night. She'd sat in her rocker crying endlessly about her dead son. Now, exhausted, she slept.

Karen wanted to find the killer. She knew that Skye Fargo was working with Tom Cain but she assumed that she could help Fargo by talking to some of her friends. Her grief would come later.

Once home, she changed from her gingham dress into her Levi's and green woolen sweater. She needed to start making candles today, not her favorite task but they were running low. She wanted to work in the large garden she'd planted. She'd been putting up vegetables for the coming winter for three months. But right now candles had to come first.

She set herself up and began the tedious process of hand-dipping. The problem was that if you topped the candle it would get too hard and would snap in two.

Somebody knocked on the door.

"Come in." She spoke softly, not wanting to wake her mother. She didn't mean to be unkind but she needed a rest from her mother's sobbing.

Ingrid Haller was a typical frontier woman. Many men were open about wanting to marry stout women because they were like having a second horse. Some women found that sentiment amusing. The slender Karen wasn't one of them and she resented the fact that men thought of women that way. Karen's outspokenness had frequently caused her trouble.

Karen put a finger to her lips. Ingrid, square-shaped in a

man's red-and-black-checkered shirt and jeans, nodded her understanding and walked over on tiptoe.

"My mother's sleeping. She had a terrible night." She nodded to the blanket strung across the rope. The two beds were on the other side.

"I'm still having a lot of terrible nights myself." Ingrid's son Michael had been the first victim of the killer.

Ingrid knew not to interrupt Karen's work. She drew up a thatched chair so she could sit close enough to talk without raising her voice. Karen continued to work.

"There's something we need to talk about, Karen."

"Oh?"

"The others don't want to talk about it and neither did I, but now I don't have any choice and neither do you."

Her bluntness surprised Karen. She had a feeling that Ingrid was going to tell her something terrible.

"It's what everybody's talking about—behind our backs."

"You're being very mysterious, Ingrid."

"You've had the same thoughts I've had but you've been afraid to admit them." The woman had a wide, pleasant, freckled face. "I don't like to think about them, either."

"Are you ever going to tell me what you're talking about?"

"I'm talking about the stagecoach robbery about a month ago. I saw my son get mad about everything right before it happened. He only acted that way when he was worried about something. I think he was worried about the robbery."

"He could've been worried about a lot of things." She kept on dipping the thin pole holding the wicks into the hot tallow.

"I don't think you're facing facts. Three of them dead right after the robbery."

"Who'd kill them?"

"Two men died in that holdup. Maybe one of their kin."

"I don't see how that could be the case. Most people would have a hard time killing three people."

Ingrid leaned back in her chair. Shook her head. "You need to be honest with yourself."

"I'm trying to be." A deep sigh. "I've thought about it, too, Ingrid."

"I figured you had. Same with Maddie about her boy. She brought it up to me. She was the one who put the idea in my head. I didn't want to believe it, either. But here we have her son, your brother and my son dead following a stagecoach robbery. And we all know how nervous they were beforehand."

"So who killed them and where's the money?"

"I don't care about the money."

"Neither do I."

"I just want whoever killed them punished."

"The worst thing is thinking about those men dying in the robbery."

"I can't believe that any of them would've done it on purpose. It had to be some kind of accident." Tears gleamed in Ingrid's blue eyes. "My son wouldn't kill anybody. I know that for sure."

Damned candles, Karen thought. She wanted to stop and relax. Confront the suspicion she'd had for several days. But they needed the candles. The winds from the mountains told of any early winter.

"What do you think about this Fargo man?" Ingrid said.

"I met him. I liked him. And I trust him."

"Tell him this. Rex Connor saw somebody talking to the three boys down by the bridge just before the first murder. At night. He was fishing when he saw them. You're a good friend of Rex."

"I sure am. I bake bread for him." Then: "People are going to turn against our kin, Ingrid."

"Let them. My boy's dead. All I care about is finding his killer. If any of those boys killed the driver and the Englishman, it had to be a mistake. They weren't killers."

"No," Karen said gently, "no, they weren't."

Karen liked the woman. A good, honest woman. And it was more and more likely that they shared a dark secret.

Ingrid reached out and the women gripped their hands together. "You talk to this Fargo. Tell him about Rex."

"I'll do that, Ingrid. Thanks."

Karen sat thinking of how strange and terrible life had become.

Fargo was walking back from the livery when he heard a bourbon-raspy voice say, "I'm afraid I was a little rude last night. At least from what I can remember, Mr. Fargo."

The voice couldn't possibly belong to anybody else in this town except for one man named O'Malley. Fargo wondered wryly if he'd ever met the man walking toward him. Now, as last night, O'Malley crept up behind him.

From what he could remember, Fargo reasoned that the man was still in the same clothes. He'd shaved but his ruddy face was a crosshatch of nicks and cuts. The eyes were as red as a matador's cape. That he was upright and ambulatory was amazing. That he spoke clearly—as if he hadn't had a drink in days—was even more startling.

"You weren't rude, O'Malley. You were just a little full of yourself. And full of a lot of rotgut whiskey, I assume."

"In my better days I drank only the best," O'Malley the leprechaun said wistfully. "But alas too much of that for my editors. They didn't understand that there is truth in the bottle."

"You mentioned that last night. A couple of times in fact. Now what can I do for you?"

People streamed around them on the wide dusty street. The way a few of the passersby winked at each other when they saw O'Malley told Fargo a lot about how the town regarded him. The town drunk, the town clown. He didn't want to feel sorry for the little bastard but he did.

"I believe I turned down your offer of cooperation."

"You did."

"Well, when I woke up this morning I thought I might think it over."

"Why's that?"

O'Malley tapped three pudgy fingers to his forehead. "As far as I can remember, when I pulled the sheets back on the bed in my dingy little hotel room there was a rattlesnake in it."

"Drunks see all sorts of things, O'Malley. Dancing girls, pink elephants—"

"If you'd care to ask the night clerk at the Excelsior hotel he'll bear out what I said. I have a distinct memory of him trapping the thing and carrying it outside. He seemed to be very dexterous with rattlesnakes. I recall being quite impressed."

Fargo studied the pudgy face. For all his grandiosity O'Malley was an intelligent man who, despite his whiskey-soaked mind, still managed to function. The story he'd told was easily enough checked. There'd be no point in lying about it. "If it's the killer he'll try again."

"And if it's the killer, I'll be waiting for him. I plan to sit up all night in my room. And I won't just have my derringer either. I own a six-gun and I know how to use it."

"Sounds like you want the killer to come at you again."

"Of course. Wouldn't you? What could be a better story than a reporter who traps a killer and gets a confession out of him?"

A dapper man in a blue suit and white shirt and red cravat came up behind O'Malley. He wore a dark Vandyke beard and a sneer. "Let me apologize to you, Mr. Fargo. My name is Amos Parrish and I'm sorry that my reporter here is no doubt wasting your time—as he wastes everybody's time in this town."

O'Malley's eyes showed embarrassment and shame as Parrish put a hand on the Irishman's shoulder.

"We were having an interesting conversation as a matter of fact," Fargo said.

"Oh, don't stick up for him. Or God knows feel sorry for him. That's his main weapon. He rooks you in and makes you become his protector. I only keep him on because every once in a while he comes up with something. But most of the time he just stumbles around town here and bores people to death with his so-called secrets. His latest secret seems to be the identity of the man who killed all three of those young men who were involved in the bank robbery. I think everybody else pretty much knows who that is but no, not O'Malley here. He knows better than everybody. He knows the 'secret.' Usually I don't interrupt him this way but I'm well aware of your reputation, Mr. Fargo, and I'm delighted that you were honorable enough to stop on your journey and bring Byrnes' body in. I'm just sorry you have to endure poor O'Malley here." He finally removed his hand from the Irishman's shoulder. "Why don't you go get yourself your morning drinks, O'Malley, and stop bothering Mr. Fargo here?"

Fargo was surprised by how quickly O'Malley turned and hurried away. His face had been scarlet with humiliation. He was a beaten man and he walked slumped over, as if he might pitch forward.

"He didn't have that coming."

"Oh, my Lord, Mr. Fargo. You weren't taken in by him, were you?"

Fargo could tell that the dapper Mr. Parrish had decided that the Trailsman might not be as impressive as he'd always heard. Skye Fargo being taken in by a drunken reporter who was on his last legs?

"I don't know that I was taken in. But you didn't need to treat him like a dog you wanted to get rid of."

The man put a fine hand on the lapel of his suit coat as if he were addressing an audience. "On my own behalf let me say that I'm his last resort. Nobody else would hire him let alone pay him for the little actual work he gets done. And I don't appreciate being called to task for how I deal with one of my employees, especially by somebody who apparently doesn't understand the circumstances. Good day to you, sir."

He stormed away. He'd be one hell of a man to work for. And once more Fargo felt a little sorry for O'Malley.

6

"Is Bob Thomas here?"

The mannish middle-aged woman in the flannel shirt raised her wide face to consider Fargo's question. She didn't appear to be taken with him at all. "Who's asking?"

"Name's Fargo."

"Oh. Heard about you. Why're you looking for Bob?"

"Need to ask him some questions."

"About what?"

The one-room office of The River Shipping Company was contained in a long crude structure made of logs. There was no back wall as such. Instead there was a loading dock. That was now piled high with boxes and crates of various sizes. From down near the shore Fargo could hear the voices of men talking and laughing as they loaded cargo.

"That would be between Thomas and me, ma'am."

"You know who I am?"

"Can't say that I do."

"I'm his mother."

"I see."

"I hired him after Lenihan fired him. My boy never stole anything."

"I need to talk to him directly, ma'am."

"If you're here about the night when he smashed the stage line window—well, that's something he shouldn't have done, even if Lenihan did fire him just because he was jealous."

"Jealous?"

"Sure. My boy Bob, all the ladies like him. Young, old,

45

don't matter. He told me she was makin' eyes at him. And he didn't start that fire, neither, in the back room after he was fired."

"I didn't hear about the fire."

"Well, he didn't do it."

Sure he didn't, Fargo thought. The little son of a bitch is a regular angel. "I need to talk to him."

The Thomas woman pushed up from her desk and said, "He's tired of people suspecting him of things." Then she walked to the dock and bellowed, "Bobby, honey, come up here, please. Man wants to talk to you."

She trundled back in, resumed her position behind her desk. "Cain probably sent you."

"I'm helping him. But he didn't send me."

"You a Pinkerton?"

"No, ma'am. But Cain seems to think I am." His humor was wasted on her.

For somebody who was loading cargo, Bob Thomas looked damned clean and shiny. He wore a fancy blue shirt, fancy blue trousers and fancy soft leather boots into which he'd tucked his fancy trousers. He had curly black hair, angry blue eyes and the kind of face some women like and all men want to damage as quickly as possible.

"Bobby's the foreman. Every job they put him on in this town they make him work like some kind of Mex or something. But I'm using him the way he should be used."

"Who the hell is this guy, Ma?"

"Now, Bobby, he just wants to ask you a few questions."

"Well, maybe I don't want to answer a few questions."

"Now, Bobby."

"I bet Cain sent you."

"Could be," Fargo said. "But you're making this a lot more difficult than it needs to be."

"Wait a minute," Thomas said. "I heard about you. You're the Trailsman or some damned name like that."

"Names don't matter. I just want to know why you were seen a couple of nights before the robbery talking to the three boys who stuck up the stage."

"That's a damn lie!"

"I've got two witnesses who'll swear to it in court."

For the first time Bobby looked to his mother for help. Fargo figured she'd probably been helping him out of situations like this all his spoiled life. "I want to get back to work, Ma."

"Mr. Fargo, if Bobby here says it's a lie—"

"Excuse us a minute, ma'am." In a single motion Fargo grabbed a handful of Thomas' fancy blue shirt and shoved him out the door. "Bobby and I'll be back in a few minutes."

The air was cooler coming off the river. The birdsong was different, too. Down on the cargo ship men moved back and forth like ants carrying their loads. Fargo pushed Thomas off the dock so that he fell two feet and landed on his bottom. He tried to scramble up but Fargo was already beside him. "Now you're going to answer my questions, sonny boy, or I'm going to break a few bones and then your ma will really have to start taking care of you."

Thomas glared up from where he still sat on his bottom. "You don't have any right—"

"What about the two witnesses who saw you with—"

Thomas snapped, "I told you that's a lie! Two nights before the robbery I wasn't even in town!"

Thomas was right. It was a lie. The Pinkertons Fargo had helped showed him how accusing somebody of something false could sometimes trick them into admitting something true.

"Then it was some other night."

He didn't need to say anything, Bobby Thomas. It was right there on his face. So he had gotten together with the three boys.

"What night was it?"

"No night. I told you."

"Get up."

"What?"

"Get up."

"What're you going to do?"

"Get up and find out."

"You're going to hit me, aren't you?"

"Yeah, and I'm going to keep on hitting you until you tell the truth. There are three boys dead. Plus an Englishman and a stagecoach driver. And maybe you know something about it."

"You don't hurt him!" Ma Thomas was now on the dock above them.

"She's got a shotgun, Fargo, and she knows how to use it."

"Well, she'd better start shooting then. Now get up!"

"Oh, shit," Thomas said. He frowned and shook his head. "I saw them one night. Two nights in fact. But I didn't have anything to do with the robbery."

"Why'd you see them?"

"The fire. I wanted them to help me." He made a face. "Can I get up now?"

"Get up."

"And you won't hit me?"

"Not if you're telling the truth."

Thomas wasn't nimble. He had to thrash around to get up. When he was upright he said, "Well, that's damn nice. Look at my pants!" He started brushing them.

His ma shouted again, "Don't you hurt him!"

"Tell her to shut up."

"She's my ma."

"Tell her." Fargo made it as menacing as possible.

"Shut up, Ma, and go back inside!"

"Well that's a fine howdy-do! You tell your own ma to shut up! See if I fix you squash the way you like it again anytime soon!"

Fargo was surprised that Thomas—who had to be twenty-five or so—didn't look embarrassed by any of this. A regular lady-killer tied tight to his mother's apron strings.

"The fire. Tell me about it."

"You going to tell Cain?"

"Not unless he asks me about it. Nobody was hurt, were they?"

"No." He actually sounded humble. "It was a stupid thing to do. I was just mad at Lenihan and mad at the three boys."

"Why were you mad at them?"

"They wouldn't help me with the fire. Which made me mad because I knew they were going to do something. They kept smiling at each other, the way you do when you've got a secret. Then all of a sudden they wanted me to leave. They got real nervous. I think somebody was coming."

"You didn't have any idea who?"

"No. And when I said something about it they got mad. Real mad. They damn near threw me on my horse they wanted to get rid of me so bad."

Fargo decided he was telling the truth, enough of it anyway. From what he'd seen of Thomas it was no wonder the boys hadn't wanted to get hooked up with him. Mama's boy. A dress-up boy for the ladies. Not somebody you'd want along on a robbery.

Thomas said, "Look at this grass stain on the side of my pants."

Fargo was well shut of him. He walked quickly back up to the office and Ma Thomas.

"I seen you throw him down." She still had the shotgun. It was pointed right at Fargo's chest.

"Maybe it's time you start throwing him down, Mrs. Thomas. He's awful old for you to still be doing his fighting."

She muttered something to his back as he left. He assumed she wasn't wishing him good luck.

Fargo had heard the worst of them called "deadfalls." And that was, in fact, what they were. Just as a deadfall was a trap for a large animal, the worst kind of saloon was also a trap. In San Francisco there were dozens of the places. A man could go into one, get drunk and wake up and find himself on a freighter bound for the China seas. All it took was for one of the saloon girls to put something in your drink and you might never be heard from again. And if the violence didn't get you the venereal disease did. A man who survived twenty-four hours on the Barbary Coast was lucky indeed. And it was in saloons like this one that the worst of the worst was found.

The Trail's End probably didn't qualify as a real deadfall but it would do until the real thing came along. After riding out to see Bob Thomas, Fargo had swung back to Cawthorne to look up a man named Frank Nolan. He was the brother of Ted Nolan, the second of the three young men to be killed.

Tom Cain wanted Fargo to carry things out the way a Pinkerton would so Fargo got Cain to write down the names of people Fargo could talk to about the dead men and how they'd spent their final days.

The Trail's End was long and narrow and lighted only by lanterns placed along the bar and at tables. Though it was barely midmorning, drunkards could be seen passed out along the bar and at one of the tables. Judging by the stench, the place could have doubled as a latrine. In the smoky lantern light, Fargo approached the crude plank bar and the beefy bald man with the black eye patch. The man's wide face reflected his displeasure with Fargo. People like the Trailsman didn't belong here. They could be law and they could most certainly be trouble.

"You lost, stranger?"

"Don't think so."

"Well, I think you are."

"Nice place you got here."

"Nobody asked you to come."

"Looking for somebody."

Eyepatch smiled. "Well, if it's anybody respectable, you sure won't find him here."

"His name is Frank Nolan."

Eyepatch's gaze flicked to the table where the man was passed out. "Never heard of him."

Fargo tossed a coin on the bar. "Beer and a shot."

Eyepatch smirked. "Cold day in hell when I serve you a damn thing."

"What the hell's that supposed to mean?"

"Means I don't like your looks. Means I don't like you standin' in front of me." He leaned forward and gave Fargo a shove.

Fargo's move was almost invisible in the shadows. He grabbed the man's right arm and twisted it with enough force to lift him up off his feet and hunched over the bar.

"Shit!" Eyepatch cried.

But Fargo didn't relent. He kept on turning the arm slowly back on itself. One of the drunkards at the bar managed to raise his head from his stupor and focus long enough to understand what was happening. And what was happening made him grin. "Looks like you met your match, Earl." Then he nudged the man slumped over to his right.

The man's head was lost beneath a wide sombrero. The enormous hat began its ascension and finally a small dark Mexican face could be seen. The face was suddenly lit by a huge smile. "Earl, man, you be in trouble."

Done with him, Fargo flung the man back against the wall, rattling the six bottles of rotgut that rested on a raw two-by-four.

"There wasn't any reason for this," Fargo said. "All I wanted was a beer and a shot."

Rubbing his arm, wincing in pain, burning with shame, Eyepatch obviously thought of saying something. But then immediately realized that Fargo might just come over the bar and start it up all over again.

"I'll take that beer and shot now."

Cursing, moving in and out of the flickering light of the lanterns, Eyepatch got Fargo what he wanted. He slammed them down hard on the bar. Fargo pitched the coin at him, grabbed his alcohol and then strode over to the table where Frank Nolan was just now sitting up and crawling out of his liquid hibernation.

He was a round little man with frightened eyes and a bad complexion. At one time his shirt had been white probably but not anymore.

"Eyepatch holds grudges, mister."

"So do I."

"I heard you askin' for me. How come?"

"Your brother."

"Oh." He was hound-dog sad suddenly. "Near to broke my ma's heart. She'll never get over it."

"My name's Fargo. I'm working with Sheriff Cain. We're trying to find out who killed your brother and the two others and why."

Nolan sat back in his chair. The move put him in deep shadow. He was almost a disembodied voice. "Glad Tom Cain's getting some help. He kinda let everybody down."

"How so?"

"Well, he didn't have no luck catchin' any of the stagecoach robbers who killed that Englishman and driver. He's usually pretty good at huntin' people down. And then right on top of it he hasn't had any luck finding out who killed my brother and them others. I try to give him the benefit of the doubt but a lot of people are sayin' maybe he's too old now. And maybe he's good with a gun but nothing else. The Denver paper's always got stories about detectives finding killers and maybe that's what we need here. I hate to see the town turn against him but with three of them dead—"

"I'm trying to find out how your brother acted the last couple days before he was killed."

"What'll that tell ya?"

"Maybe nothing. But maybe you or somebody else will remember something he might have said or done that would tell us something—maybe somebody was after him. Something like that."

Nolan yawned. He was half-sober after his sleep but he was still in the process of waking up. "There was just that one night, I guess."

"What night?"

Another yawn. "I need some fresh air."

"Right now I need you to talk to me."

"How about I take that shot of yours?"

"Fine by me if you'll keep talking."

"I'm not a drunkard. It's just my kid brother's death and all—"

For some reason Fargo believed him. He shoved the shot glass across the table.

"Thank you." Nolan belted it back.

"Tell me about your brother and that night you mentioned."

"There's this creek where we fish. I was bedding down the horses when I seen him come up from there and he looked madder than hell. I asked him what was wrong but he wouldn't tell me. But then when he got in the light I could see that his jaw was red and swollen."

"Somebody hit him."

"Sure looked that way. So I went down there. To the water. Looked around. I could see somebody up against the foothills, ridin' away."

"But no idea who?"

"Too far away."

"Your brother ever mention it again?"

"No. He kind of kept to himself. Especially after his friend got killed. Ma got scared. She kept beggin' him to talk because something was wrong. You could see it all over his face." Then he shook his head. Miserably. "Then he got killed, too." Was that a sob? Fargo wondered. "I usually do day work, anything that comes along. Me and another fella, there's enough work to support us all right except in the worst of winter. I should be workin' now. But I haven't felt like it. And it's hard to go home. Facin' my ma. She's of the notion that since I was his older brother I should have taken care of him. And you know the hell of it?"

"What's that?"

"I sort of feel the same way myself. Guilty. Maybe that's why all I want to do is sit in this shithole and get drunk."

Fargo put money on the bar for more drinks.

"How was your brother acting before he got killed?"

"Funny. He'd jump at every noise. And I'd always see him staring off like he was really trying to think something through. But mostly I noticed how nervous he was. He'd never been like that before and I grew up with him. I asked him about it and asked him why he was so scared. But he just blew up—started shouting at me that he was fine and that his business was his business and that I was to stay out of it."

"Did you see him the day he disappeared?"

"No."

"I'm at the Royale for the next twenty-four hours. In and out. If you think of something leave a note for me there."

"Eyepatch'll have to write it."

"How's that?"

"Never learned to write."

Eyepatch had been listening to it all, of course. "Next time you call this place a shithole, Frank, you can take your business someplace else. I worked hard to get this place up to snuff."

Fargo did the man a favor. He didn't laugh out loud.

It was a town of cowboys and miners and greenhorns, of outriders and homesteaders and drummers. And gunfighters and cardsharps and slickers. And as recently as a month ago Cawthorne had been the private domain of Sheriff Tom Cain. He had tamed it and he made sure it stayed tamed. Most of the good citizens here both liked him and respected him. And even those who hated him were forced to respect him.

Cain walked among the wagons and buggies and horses and mules that filled the main street. He didn't much care for the looks he got this morning, though. Few smiled, most hurried past him on his walk to the courthouse. They would usually have stopped to pay their respects. But there were three dead young men and it was pretty much agreed that Sheriff Tom Cain really didn't have any idea who was behind their murders.

Amy Peters knew these things about Sheriff Tom Cain because he had expressed each and every one of them to her over the years. When he had first begun thrusting himself on her, shortly after his arrival, he had been all strutting male, smirking at the notion that she would someday be Ned Lenihan's bride. She'd never liked him and liked him less with each passing year. But he was the most important man in Cawthorne, even more important than the three men on the town council, and for the sake of her children she needed to be pleasant.

These days he tried a gentler approach. He talked to her as if she were his confidante. Told her about his doubts instead of his triumphs. But like most things with Tom Cain, it was calculated. If he couldn't get her one way, he'd just try another.

She thought of this as she watched him approach the buggy she had just stepped down from. This was her twice-weekly visit to the general store. No matter how she tried to vary the times she arrived, Cain somehow always appeared.

His rugged face broke into a smile that he knew well made him even handsomer. He tipped his hat, too. She was getting the whole show.

"I knew something good would happen to me today if I just held on long enough," he said.

"Morning, Tom."

"Going to Herb's?"

"As usual."

"Just the shopping basket?"

He referred to the wicker basket on the arm of her dark blue blouse. "Just a few staples."

"Mind if I walk with you?"

"Would it make any difference if I did?"

A forced laugh. "You know, I've told you how sorry I am that I was such a fool about everything."

She sighed. Maybe he was sincere after all. Nobody could be insincere all the time. "Let's walk, Tom."

Before he could speak, a man shouted at Cain, "You're doin' a good job, Tom! Don't let 'em tell you no different!"

"Thanks, Cornelius! Appreciate it!"

"Well, nice to know I've got one person still backin' me up." He placed the white Stetson back on his head and said, "I know some of the people have turned against me. But I've got an old friend of mine, man named Skye Fargo, helping me. He's worked with the Pinkertons a couple times."

"Never knew you to ask for help before."

"Maybe I'm not the man you think I am."

"I remember all the terrible things you said about Ned."

"I remember them, too, Amy, and I'm sorry about that too. The old green-eyed beast had me in its clutches was all. Here I was a big strapping town tamer and Lenihan's a nice decent man. But I guess I've read too many yellowbacks. Not all women want a town tamer for a husband. And I admire you for standing by him with his problems with the bank and all."

Poor Ned, she thought. He'd been so aggrieved lately. One night he couldn't even make love. She worried about him—worried about them as a couple. Ned didn't want to get married until he paid off his farm. And the robbery had obviously placed him under some suspicion. Once it was known that there had been a secret shipment of money on that stagecoach where the Englishman and driver had been murdered, people naturally began to suspect everybody at the stage line office. But suspecting Ned was ridiculous. No matter what kind of financial trouble he was in there was no way he'd ever throw in with stage robbers.

"There's a lot you don't know about me, Amy. Maybe there's a lot more you *need* to know before you run off and do something foolish."

They had reached the general store. Three women stood on the plank walk, their gingham bonnets tilted toward one another conspiratorially. Amy assumed they must be gossiping. Gossiping was sinful but it sure could be fun.

She raised her dark eyes to his and said, "I love Ned. He's a good man. My children love him. They already treat him like a father. Nothing's going to change that, Tom. Nothing. I appreciate your apologies but nothing's going to change that."

"Well, unaccustomed as I am to losing the lady I've pursued, I have to say that I've been wrong about you and Lenihan. I can see that you're going to have a good marriage."

She would have been more inclined to believe him if he hadn't worn that sharklike grin. The grin that said he was superior to all he surveyed. "Good-bye, Tom."

She stood there watching him go. For all his kind words, he'd managed to remind her of Ned's financial difficulties—another way of saying that Ned had a good reason to get his hands on some of that robbery money.

But as she entered the general store with her wicker basket, she wondered. Why had his words troubled her so much?

"Won't give you no more credit, O'Malley. You want a drink, I want to see some money."

O'Malley called it his shoe money. Aptly named. Tucked under the insole of his boot was enough money to get him drunk for a night. Whatever else his expenses might be, he always took care to replenish his shoe money so that in an emergency the money would always be there. And this he considered an emergency—an emergency of the soul. Parrish took pleasure in humiliating O'Malley as often as possible, knowing that the reporter couldn't quit. He survived on the pittance Parrish paid him. But never before had he been humiliated in front of the likes of the Trailsman. The legendary figure so many other journalists had written about.

He had gone back to his shabby hotel room and tried to sleep. The ultimate escape. But sleep hadn't come because he ran out of whiskey. Only large amounts of whiskey could put him into the blissful darkness of slumber. Otherwise all he did was lie there and relive his wasted and terrible life. All the things he could have been—but ended up here in Cawthorne.

Finally he'd gotten up, put on his clothes and come here to the Gilded Cage, the only saloon that had ever consented to give him credit. He figured that if he was going to spend money he owed it to this saloon to spend it here.

At this time of day the place was only half full. The men ran to old-timers who played cards and gossiped and talked politics. One other reason he came here is that he'd never been made fun of. At least not that he could remember. The crowd here didn't seem to have any interest in him at all. He'd stand at the far end of the bar where Aaron, the owner, usually took care of business, and nobody bothered him.

"You don't have to worry about me, Aaron," O'Malley said. "I've got plenty of money." He'd taken his money from the shoe before coming here. He'd give people a nasty laugh for sure if he took it out here. He laid some greenbacks on the bar and said, "That should take care of what I owe you and buy me some whiskey and a schooner of beer."

Aaron Cade, a golden bear of a man with broad shoulders and hair so blond it was almost white, smiled and said, "You come into some money, did you, O'Malley?"

"Not yet. But soon."

"Oh? You got an inheritance or something?"

O'Malley knew he probably shouldn't say anything but after suffering Parrish's mocking words, he wanted to feel important again. "No, no inheritance. A story I'm working on. When this one comes out that Denver paper'll be wiring me to come back."

"You sure of that?" Aaron's tone wasn't unkind, just gently doubtful.

"Money in the bank," O'Malley laughed. "And I mean that both ways. Money in the bank that the story's going to be that great. And money in the bank that that's what I'll have—money in the bank and plenty of it."

"For your sake, I hope you're right, O'Malley."

Aaron went to take care of one of the oldsters at a card table. The man's back had been seriously damaged in a mining accident about ten years ago. He needed help getting up out of his chair and aimed in the general direction of the outhouse in back of the saloon.

O'Malley watched Aaron guide the old man. That was a warning sign to him. He didn't want to wake up one day and find himself in the same situation this older man did. O'Malley's dream was of the life he'd led in the big cities before the bottle had taken over his life so completely. There

58

had been fresh young women and expensive meals in fashionable restaurants and spring days when he felt confident that someday he'd not only be working for a newspaper, he'd be running one.

When Aaron returned, O'Malley ordered another round for himself. He ordered a shot for Aaron, too. The bartender smiled. "You down to your shoe money?"

"My shoe money? How'd you know about that?"

"You told me one night."

God. So hard to remember what he said and did. Had to be careful with his secret. Had to be very careful. "Well, do me a favor and keep it to yourself."

"Won't do any good, O'Malley."

"And why's that?"

"Same night you told me you told about half the people in here the same thing. I was surprised somebody didn't wait for you outside and take your shoe off. I hate to admit it but some of my customers ain't exactly saints. They hear of a drunk with a shoe full of money—"

O'Malley laughed but it was forced. "Me and my big mouth, huh?"

"You got to be careful. I don't know what kind of thing you're talking about—something big obviously—but you better watch yourself when you're drinking. Don't want to give it away."

Aaron moved down the bar to grab a couple of empty schooners and clean up.

O'Malley's heady dreams had been dashed for the moment. Aaron was right. O'Malley always ran his mouth when he was drunk. Had he already told somebody what he had figured out?

But then his hand dipped into the pocket of his soiled suit coat. Merely touching it filled him with hope once again. He took it out and laid it on the bar momentarily, far from the eyes of Aaron. He just looked at it. To the uneducated eye this wouldn't look like much at all. In fact, the uneducated eye would pass right by it. But to O'Malley this was Chicago and St. Lou all over again. Those fancy meals and those fancier girls.

He sat there staring at it, the silver button that was a match to the one Fargo had found near the body of Clete Byrnes.

7

Sam Raines was the first one down from the second floor of Rose Fitzhugh's Parlor of Pleasure. Early in the day for sex but then it was also early for drinking four shots of whiskey back to back.

He had just enjoyed the pleasures of a buxom redhead who had tasted of the perfume she had put on the hottest part of her body and who had enjoyed—or who had faked enjoying—the mating as much as he had. She had worn a sheer black slip under which her full breasts had shifted with mesmerizing grace. Her nipples were enormous and red-tipped like spring flowers.

He had been rough with her at first, pushing her back on the bed and trying to jam himself inside her before she was properly damp. But she had quickly educated, easing him out and gently putting him on his back where she'd begun to stroke his manhood with educated and nimble fingers. He had been ready to explode then but those educated fingers had dissuaded him from ending their session so abruptly. And somehow he found himself pleasuring her, his mouth on her womanliness, and enjoying the joy he was giving her. But once again she stopped when she sensed that he was ready to end things. She got up on her haunches so he could take her from the rear—as he'd whispered his wishes earlier—and in that position gave him the kind of sexing he'd rarely enjoyed. He'd certainly gotten his money's worth.

He was buttoning up his trousers when the plump Rose, a gaudy wreck of a woman who affected red wigs and enough makeup to cover a line of six high-kicking saloon dancers, came through the beaded curtain leading to the parlor where the customers sat. As usual she carried a meerschaum pipe in one hand and a fancy fan in the other. She smoked the clay pipe frequently. "What's wrong with that brother of yours this morning?"

"What the hell business is it of yours?"

"It's my business when he hits one of my girls."

"They're whores, what's the difference?"

"He never hit none of them before, not even when he was drunk. I'm wonderin' what's botherin' him."

Sam knew damned well what was bothering Kenny. Kenny Raines, the blond and more handsome of the brothers, was worried about the same thing Sam was.

"You have one of your gals get me a whiskey and you never mind what's troubling him."

She looked at him with aged agate-colored eyes. But there was a youthful impishness in her gaze now. She was enjoying this. "Never thought I'd see the Raines brothers worried about anything."

"You get out of my sight, Rose."

She fluttered her fan in front of her wrinkled doll-like face, parted the beaded curtain and went into the other area of the house.

He got up and walked to the window that looked out on the butt end of the town. To his mind, one long latrine. People still living in tents and shanties. On the other side of the mud street were the saloons and the casinos, the owners of which lived in Cawthorne proper. No way would they live here among the people they hired for pennies a day. This was where respectable people and visitors came to be bad and as soon as they'd taken their pleasure they hightailed out of here.

The whorehouse was quiet, something Sam wasn't used to. A Negro man with enormous pink arm garters usually played the piano. A girl or two in filmy dresses carried trays of drinks around. On nights when the wait was long you might find three or four customers playing a friendly hand of poker.

The beaded curtain parted. A middle-aged Mexican woman with large hands gave him his drink. "Your brother, he was bad with Deborah this morning." She touched her eye. "The black eye as it is called."

What the hell was this? First Rose and now this Mex. They acted like no girl ever got slugged before in a whorehouse. He'd been going to whorehouses since he was fourteen. Girls got slugged in them all the time.

The curtains rattled again and there was his brother. The Mex scowled at him. Kenny laughed. "She giving you shit about that little gal upstairs?"

"Says you gave her a black eye."

"Yeah, well she probably gave me crabs. So we're even up." He raised his bandaged hand. "All I did was backhand the bitch with this."

The Mex flashed a look that said he was despicable and left.

Kenny walked over and took Sam's drink from him. Took a deep swallow and handed it back. "You been thinking about it?"

"I don't know what we should do. This Fargo—"

"Right now he's all I care about."

Kenny purloined his brother's drink again. Took another deep swallow and handed it back. Sam hadn't taken a drink yet. "If you won't help me, I'll do it alone."

"He's thrown in with Cain."

"To hell with Cain. People want rid of him anyway. It ain't like the old days when he was such a big man."

The beads clattered again. Rose. She said, "It's one thing hittin' a girl at night. At least I can understand that a little bit. But hittin' a girl this early in the day, I should charge you boys double."

"You're lucky we didn't hit *you*, Rose," Kenny said.

Then he whipped the drink from his brother's hand and finished it. He handed the empty glass to Rose.

"C'mon, Sam, let's get the hell out of here."

It was only as they were walking out that Sam Raines realized he hadn't gotten as much as a sip of his own drink.

Fargo stood behind three people in line for stagecoach tickets. This gave him a chance to observe Ned Lenihan. The Pinks he'd worked with said that you could tell a lot about a man just by watching him deal with other people. If he was in any kind of trouble he might appear agitated in some way.

If Lenihan was agitated, he knew how to keep it hidden.

"The finest book I've ever read," said a sensible-looking middle-aged woman in a man's denim shirt and gray butternuts. She held the book up for Lenihan to see. "*Uncle Tom's Cabin.* Have you ever read it, Ned?"

"No. But I've been meaning to. Amy has and she really enjoyed it."

"I'm taking it along on my trip to Denver. That's one of the few good things about the stagecoach—no offense, Ned—I get a lot of reading done. Unless the other people talk too loud. You get some real loud ones once in a while."

Lenihan was a small man of about forty with fine, precise features. Instead of looking annoyed at the woman prattling on when there were other customers waiting, his smile seemed to say that he really enjoyed her company. All the while he was making out her ticket.

"Yep, I'll read it through again and then I'll give it to my granddaughter. She's eight but she can read up a storm. She'll love it as much as I do."

The next two customers were just as talkative and Lenihan was just as patient. He stood there in his blue shirt with the black bolo tie, able to watch them as he scribbled out their fares.

Fargo knew you couldn't judge a man by either appearance or demeanor. He'd once hunted a grandfatherly man who had set fire to his daughter and three grandchildren. Their offense was trying to stop him from playing his accordion late at night. The man had a face that would have worked as a magazine illustration of all that was right and good and wise of old age.

But if Lenihan had killed three men in cold blood he had a kind of cunning that Fargo had never encountered before. Cold-blooded killer in the night, friendly open man during the day.

Then it was Fargo's turn to step up to the counter.

"Howdy. Can I help you?"

"Name's Skye Fargo. I'm helping Tom Cain." He wasn't surprised to see Lenihan's face tighten. He had to know he was under suspicion for the robbery.

"Yessir. What can I do for you?"

"Wanted to talk to you about that robbery last month."

"Terrible. That Englishman was headed back home when it happened and the driver was a good friend of mine."

"I was thinking more about the money that got stolen, I guess." Fargo kept his gaze fixed on the man's face. "I'm told you were one of the few people who knew about it."

"I guess that makes me guilty, huh?" Anger, frustration.

"I didn't say that. I'm not making any accusations. I'm just trying to find out what happened."

"I heard you were helping Cain. In case you didn't know, he spent a good bit of time trying to win my woman from me."

"He told me that he'd given up."

"So he says. And here's something else you might think about. Tom Cain knew about that shipment, too."

"You're saying that he had something to do with it?"

"I'm saying that since the rest of us are under suspicion, he should be too. And personally, I don't know why you'd want to get hooked up with a man like Cain."

"I'm doing him a favor. He's an old friend of mine."

"Favor, huh? By my lights he's a bully and a liar." He smiled. "You know what this is about? He wants to marry the woman I plan to marry. It'd be one thing if she wanted to marry him. I'd step aside. I wouldn't want to force her into anything. I'm not like that. But Cain'll do anything. And I guess I should've figured he'd come up with something like this. Like saying I was in cahoots with those robbers or something. He gets me in trouble and then he has a clear field with Amy. Or that's what he thinks anyway. But I know better. I'm sure if I was out of the picture Amy would find another man—she's very pretty and very healthy—but it wouldn't be Tom Cain. Not under any circumstances I can think of."

"That a serious accusation or you just talking?"

Deep sigh. "I don't know. I hate Cain and I'd like to see him run out of town. Or sent to prison. He made out real good taming this town. So I got to admit I may just be talking. But I've thought about it and I can't see who else it would've been that tipped off those robbers. Maybe somebody at the other end, at the bank. But there's no way for me to know that since I don't know any of the people over there. And besides, if it was somebody over there I'd think the president of the bank would have his suspicions and he hasn't said anything. And he's been over here twice. So as far as I'm concerned that leaves Cain."

"So you are accusing Cain of robbery and murder."

Lenihan had an easy smile. "And you know what? I don't have any trouble sleeping and I digest my food just fine."

The door opened and a fetching young woman in a yellow blouse, a brown leather vest and Levi's walked in. Her body was rich with curves. Breasts turned the yellow blouse into a fine tribute to femininity. Fargo didn't recognize her at first. The first and only time he'd seen her it had been night and she was dressed in funeral black. Sarah Friese, the undertaker's daughter.

"Howdy, Ned."

"Howdy yourself, Sarah."

"I've got this box I need to send to Fox Junction. No hurry but thought I'd drop it off here." She came over and set it on the counter. Looked like a cigar box, wrapped in tan paper, string neatly enclosing it.

"I'll get you a receipt," Ned said.

While he went to work, she looked at Fargo. "You probably don't recognize me."

"I sure do."

"My father says that I don't have to worry about men chasing me as long as I keep wearing his funeral clothes."

"Hard to mistake a good-looking woman even in funeral clothes."

She touched Fargo's arm with long, thin fingers. "Did you hear that, Ned? There should be more men like him in Cawthorne. Maybe my father could get me married off after all." Then: "I hope to see you soon, Mr. Fargo."

"I have a feeling you probably will."

She favored each man with another smile and left.

As soon as she was gone, Lenihan jabbed a finger in the air. "I didn't have one damn thing to do with that robbery. Nothing. And like I told you, as far as I'm concerned this is nothing more than Cain trying to steal Amy from me. Now I'd appreciate it if you'd get the hell out of here."

Fargo was ten steps from the stage line office when he saw Deputy Pete Rule standing near an ore wagon talking to a couple of men. He headed over there, standing back until Rule was finished with his conversation. Rule didn't look all that happy to see him.

"Heard you signed on, Fargo."

"For twenty-four hours."

"Glad to hear it. I've been doing some nosing around myself."

"I got tricked into it. I wanted to be on my way to Denver now. I'm doing this as a favor to the three women who asked me. Cain put them up to it but I'm doing it anyway—for twenty-four hours. And then I'm gone whether I find out anything or not. Just because I'm asking around doesn't mean you have to stop. The thing is to find the killer. Doesn't matter much who finds him."

"Well, I'll keep asking around."

"One thing I'm trying to figure out is Cain and this woman Amy Peters. I just talked with Ned Lenihan. He seems to think that Cain wants to blame the robbery and the killings on Lenihan so he can have Amy all to himself."

Rule smiled, looking younger and healthier. "Well, she's a beauty. No doubt about that. But Tom, he gave up on her a while back. It got embarrassing for everybody. He really tried everything he could to win her over and a lot of people hated him for it. Ned Lenihan doesn't compare to a big good-looking man like Cain. And Ned's a local man, so naturally most of the people took his part. And I think the sheriff took about all the humiliation he could. She made it real plain that she was in love with Ned and standing by him and that Cain didn't have a chance. So he gave up."

"So Lenihan's wrong?"

"About Cain still chasing after Amy, yes. But Ned has financial troubles with his farm. That means he needs money. He doesn't want to talk about that. That's why Cain thinks he might have arranged the robbery with those three boys. He needs the money. But he can't fool people into believing that Cain is just after him because of Amy."

"What's your opinion?"

Rule's leathery face wrinkled into a frown. "That's the thing. I like Ned. He's a hard worker and a decent man. But the trouble is he loves that little farm of his almost as much as he loves Amy. So if it came down to setting up a robbery to save it"—he sighed—"well, I haven't made up my mind yet."

"Thanks, Pete. I'm glad we got to have this talk."

"Yeah," Rule said. And damned if he didn't smile again. That was two in the space of a few minutes. Maybe he wasn't just a sour cuss after all. "Now I don't have to go around sulking all day."

A large red barn stood next to a rope corral where six horses stood while a Cheyenne man examined them. Inside the barn came the sounds of stagecoaches being repaired and made ready for the torture of traveling over roads that could seriously damage or even destroy any stagecoach ever made. Fargo had swung back here after talking to Rule. He'd talked to Lenihan. He decided it was time to talk to Kenny Raines and his brother Sam. As employees of the stage line, they'd known about the money in the strongbox, too.

He stood at the edge of the barn and peered into the cool shadows inside. A stout bald man with a red beard shaped like a dagger stepped away from a wheel he was inspecting, wiped his hands on a leather apron and said, "Help you?"

"Looking for the Raines brothers."

The man came out into the sunlight. "Say, aren't you that Fargo?"

"Yep."

"You shot up Kenny's hand last night."

"Didn't have much choice."

"That's what gunnies always say."

"Didn't know I was a gunny."

"That's what they always say, too. Those boys are friends of mine. Sam stood up for my boy at his Confirmation last year."

"Are they here?"

"Hell, no, they're not here. Kenny's hand is all wrapped up. He was at the doc's for three or four hours last night thanks to you."

"Where can I find them?"

"You gonna shoot him again?"

"Thought I'd use a bow and arrow this time."

"I don't think you're so funny."

Fargo remembered something one of the Pinkertons had told him. About half the people you spoke to trying to get to the truth would dislike you. A few might hate you. Fargo had just met somebody in the latter category.

"Where can I find them? I won't ask again."

"You gonna shoot me, too?"

"Won't need to. I can handle you with my fists."

For a man who appeared slow and sluggish, he sprang at Fargo with speed and accuracy. He rammed into the Trails-man, big hands going for Fargo's throat. A bad mistake. Just as the man's fingers were about to close on Fargo's throat, the Trailsman brought a fist up from his waist and slammed it under the man's chin. For a few seconds the man continued to reach for Fargo but then without any warning his eyes rolled back into his head and he staggered backward. Fargo went after him, a crashing right hand to the man's left cheek, a left to the man's ribs.

By now a half-dozen workmen stood at the barn door watching as Fargo reached down and hauled the man to his feet. The workmen didn't want any part of it. The man's face was bruised. His lips were covered with blood. His eyes flicked about, trying to focus.

"Now I'm going to ask you some questions and you're going to answer them. You hear me?"

The man sobbed a few words but didn't answer.

Fargo shook him. "You hear me?"

"You better answer, Red. He's gonna kick your ass if you don't." This came from one of the workmen.

Another workman laughed. "Looks to me like he already got his ass kicked."

"Now he knows what it feels like," a third man said. "Maybe he'll stop pickin' on us now."

Fargo said, "Where can I find them?"

Red glared at him. He was apparently a bully. He'd been humiliated in front of the men he'd bullied. "Probably the Gold Mine."

"You think they had anything to do with that robbery?"

Red had gathered himself enough to sneer. "Hell, no, they didn't, Fargo. Everybody knows who set that up and who's been killing those boys."

"Who would that be?"

"Right up there in the front office." He nodded. "Ned Lenihan. He thinks because he puts on a good face for everybody and because he's got that widow woman he can get away with anything. But he's wrong. Somebody's gonna prove he did it and then there'll be hell to pay."

"That's right, mister," one of the workmen called. "We figure it had to be Ned. He's smart and he'd know how to set it up. Way we figure it, it couldn't have been anybody else."

Ned Lenihan. Fargo had learned one thing anyway. A

good share of the folks around here figured Lenihan was behind it all. But that was another thing the Pinkertons had taught him. The obvious suspect wasn't always the guilty party. Sometimes the obvious one was actually a distraction. You could spend all your time and energy trying to prove he was the culprit while the real culprit got away.

"Next time somebody asks you a question, Red, you better decide if you want to answer it or get your ass whipped." Fargo shoved him away so hard that Red fell on his backside. Then Fargo walked away.

8

O'Malley had learned how to pick door locks back in Chicago. A colored man who'd given him information on another story had idly boasted that he could open any door lock presented him in under sixty seconds. O'Malley had been amused by the bragging and offered the man money if he could open four doors of O'Malley's choosing. And damned if the man hadn't been able to do it. One thing that O'Malley had noticed was how the thief always kept his back to O'Malley so the reporter couldn't see what he was doing exactly. Later, when they were drinking beer in a colored bar, the man had laid out several small picks on the table. A few of them looked like things a dentist would use. These, the man explained, were burglary tools. He also explained that for the right price he'd sell these same tools to O'Malley. The reporter didn't need to be convinced. He emptied his pockets and took them home. The business of reporting was a competitive one. To get a better story than another reporter you needed all the help you could get. And what if you had the power to get into any house, any flat, any business office? What kind of reporter would that make you?

Unfortunately, O'Malley's skills with burglary tools conflicted with his skills as a drinker. In both Chicago and St. Lou he'd managed to get into many a home and many a business office. One of the problems he had was that he got so drunk after looking around that he lost his notebook or forgot what he'd learned. And in both cities the burglary tools led to similar incidents that got him fired. One incident was in a fancy Chicago hotel room. After he'd been inside for a time, trying to find evidence that the girl who lived there was the mistress of a powerful alderman, he discovered the liquor cabinet and drank himself into unconsciousness and passed out on the floor. He was discovered and the paper fired him. Pretty much the same thing in St. Lou except that this was the home of a corrupt banker who found him sleeping peacefully on the couch. The banker threatened to sue the newspaper if O'Malley wasn't fired.

All these memories came flooding back as O'Malley stood in front of this door in this town now. His plan was to make certain that he could gather enough evidence on the killer. And then he would go to Parrish and tell the bastard only one thing—that he could break the story here or that he could sell it to a Denver paper. The folks in Denver lived every day to find out what was going on in Cawthorne. These murders were more intriguing than any murders presently happening in Denver. And papers large and small thrived on murder stories, didn't they?

He was just bending down to begin trial and error with his burglary tools when he heard somebody coming. Jamming the tools in the small leather case he carried for them, he hurried down to the end of the hall that opened on another hallway. He could hide there to see who was coming.

The killer. Or the person he was pretty sure was the killer.

He pressed himself flat against the wall. No sense peeking around the edge of the wall. He knew who it was and knew where the person was going. Key in lock. Door being pushed inward. Footsteps going inside. The door closing.

O'Malley had a sudden need for a smoke but wondered if it would be foolish to roll one and enjoy it. To help him think through this problem he reached in his hip pocket and retrieved his metal flask. God bless his metal flask. In the good old days when he was just starting out in Chicago his lady fair of the moment—and fair she'd been indeed—had given it to him for Christmas. Inscribed: With Love, Sharon. Somehow through all the turbulence of his life he'd managed to hang on to it. He'd never lost it or hocked it, though the latter had come to mind many times in the course of the years. It was real silver and pawnshops would pay a fair price for it.

The whiskey felt good going down, even better as it began to burn up into his chest and throat. Salvation and nothing less. Then he checked the railroad watch he'd bought a week ago. Railroad watches he lost frequently. He'd give the person fifteen minutes to walk out of the building and go away. If this didn't happen O'Malley would come back later.

He rolled a cigarette and lighted it up. As he started fanning away the smoke he heard the door open in the other hall. What if the person decided to use his hall as a way of leaving? O'Malley cursed himself for his stupidity. What would he say? What could he say? I just happen to be standing in this hall smoking a cigarette for no particular reason? If the person really was the killer, O'Malley's excuse would sound ridiculous and the killer would be on to him immediately.

But luck was with O'Malley for once. The door was closed, the key turned to lock it. And the footsteps led away, taking the same path they'd taken before.

O'Malley was so delighted with his luck he decided there was only one way to congratulate himself for his cunning. He took one, two more swigs—and big swigs they were— from the silver flask and then he peeked around the corner.

All clear.

Straightening his suit coat and shirt, pulling down his vest, O'Malley strode down the hall to the just-vacated room. He had to caution himself to be careful. Somebody else could come along.

He took out his burglary tools and set to work. It took him three tries to get the door open and then, just as it opened, he heard somebody else entering the hall just as the possible killer had. What to do? He hurried inside and closed the door as quietly as possible. Then he once again flattened himself against the wall. What if something had been forgotten and the footsteps meant the person was coming back? Not even an implausible excuse would work for this one. He could be jailed for breaking and entering, the great danger of doing your reporting this way.

The footsteps came closer. O'Malley's desire was to have another go with the flask but what if in his nervous state he dropped it?

O'Malley held his breath as the footsteps reached the door. People died of heart attacks, didn't they? Would this be his time? And then the steps went on by.

He proceeded to go through the room. He had been here once before and that was when he found the coat with the silver button. Unfortunately, he'd heard somebody coming down the hall and panicked. He raced from the room before he had time to go through everything. Today he planned to look at everything carefully.

He'd done enough police reporting to know how coppers went through rooms. How they not only lifted up cushions and pillows but felt inside them to see if anything had been hidden in them. The same with clothes in closets. The same with rugs that needed to be lifted to see what might be hidden under them.

He found a number of things under the couch cushions. Coins, combs, halves of opry house tickets, even a magazine. But none of these told him anything. The same with the cardboard wardrobe in the corner. Nothing special about the clothes at all. And nothing special in their pockets. He went through shoes and boots. Nothing inside them either. Frustrated, he went to a stack of magazines and started turning them upside down to see if something might drop out. Pieces of tobacco, a candy wrapper, another opry house ticket stub.

There were only three framed paintings on the wall. All frontier depictions. He took them down, felt along the backs, found nothing. It was while he was looking at the last painting that his eye settled on the bottom of the armchair and the space underneath. He'd checked the armchair along with everything else but what he hadn't done was look under the armchair. Shouldn't be difficult, just push it aside.

The chair was covered in a red-and-black design. He nudged against one arm of it and pushed it back far enough so that he could see the floor. Nothing to see but some dust devils and a few magazine pages that had been torn out and collected under the chair. He looked at the pages for some sort of clue to prove his theory but if they had some significance he couldn't find it.

The failure was getting to him so he stopped for another drink. He thought of smoking in here but that would be too dangerous. What if he accidentally burned something? A telltale sign that somebody had been in here.

He capped the flask and shoved it in his back pocket. And this time his gaze fell on the couch. He didn't hold out much hope—this whole excursion felt now like a total failure—but what the hell. He'd leave after this and try to think of another way to prove his suspicions.

He walked over to the couch. This took more effort to move than a simple nudge. He bent down and began pushing it out of its position. It was heavier than it looked, the claw feet and all the wood in the structure giving it real weight. He had only turned the couch halfway beyond its previous point when he saw it. A shallow box about the size of a magazine. A feminine blue lid with a lighter blue bottom. He reached down and picked it up. Given the room's dust, he had to blow a coat of gray from the lid. He took the flask from his pocket, dropped it on the couch and then seated himself to open the box and examine its contents.

The rather stiffly posed photograph on top told him that his suspicions had been correct. There had been a link between the robbery of the woman's house and the killer. He looked through a trove of illicit obsessions. More posed photographs, two locks of hair, a fine handkerchief, a delicate comb and three or four newspaper articles. But the letters were what held his interest. They were love letters that had never been sent. Their passion, their yearning, their blunt vulnerability—who would suspect any of this in the person O'Malley now knew to be the killer? He went through the unsent letters twice, practically memorizing one of them. He could imagine them on the front page of a newspaper. One per issue. He could imagine how they would be talked about.

How they would be mocked by some, secretly cherished by others. He could imagine the editors of powerful newspapers saying that they must get in touch with the man who wrote these stories. They must have him on staff. And they would agree to just about any salary he asked for. Yes, what a great element these letters would make when the killer had been unmasked and these letters were quoted in O'Malley's stories about the strange and sad events in little Cawthorne, Colorado. This story had everything that readers wanted.

He sat back and lifted the flask to his mouth. As he was closing the box, he saw the edge of something he had somehow missed in the corner of a group of recipes and church bulletins he had not bothered to look through. There'd been enough of them that he hadn't noticed it till now.

He lifted the papers and there it was. He stared at it as if he'd discovered one of those mythic treasures writers so loved to write about—pirates' gold or a lost work of art. But in this case it was more valuable than either.

A posed photograph of Ned Lenihan with his face slashed several times.

He closed the box and left quickly, more excited than he'd been since his days in St. Lou.

At one o'clock in the afternoon the Gold Mine was only half full. Instead of the gamblers who collected here at night the card players were older men playing not poker but pinochle. There were sandwiches of beef and bread on the bar. The piano was quiet and there was no sign of girls. Fargo didn't have trouble spotting Kenny Raines. He sat at a table with a glass of beer in front of him glaring at Fargo. His gun hand was bandaged. The younger man sitting next to him, with the same bulbous nose and freckled face, was obviously his younger brother. He glared too but he couldn't summon the same intensity as his brother.

The day bartender, a beanpole of a man in a vivid yellow shirt and red arm garters, took it all in and reached beneath the bar. Fargo saw the move and said, "There won't be any trouble."

"The hell there won't," Kenny Raines shouted. He started to stand but his brother reached up and yanked him back down.

"You don't have a gun hand, Kenny," Sam said, reminding Kenny of the obvious. But it was clear to Fargo that Kenny had been doing a lot of drinking for this time of day.

The card players had stopped to watch. Not only were they interested in the possible gunplay—they wanted to scatter if they needed to. One curious thing about saloon shootouts was that the victims often had nothing to do with the fight itself. They just hadn't been able to get out of the way fast enough.

Fargo walked over to the table where the brothers sat. He grabbed a chair and sat down.

"This hand's gonna get healed, Fargo. And then I'm comin' after you."

Fargo looked at Sam. "Tell your brother by the time this hand heals I'll be long gone. Also tell him that all I want to do is ask you a few questions. Both of you."

"You shot his hand."

"I shot his hand because he was drunk and started a fight with me."

"Me and him and Clete were good friends."

"Then I'm talking to the right people."

"What's that supposed to mean?"

"Don't talk to that son of a bitch, Sam," Kenny said, waving his white-wrapped hand as if willing Fargo out of existence.

"It means two things. It means that because you knew in advance about that money shipment, you're both suspects."

"That's a damned lie. We didn't have nothing to do with it!" Now Fargo had riled Sam, too.

"And it also means that since you were such good friends with Clete, maybe you can tell me if he said anything to you after the robbery. And how he was acting. If he'd changed a lot all of a sudden."

Sam looked at Kenny. "I guess it won't hurt to talk, Kenny." Then back to Fargo. "But we didn't have nothing to do with it, like I said, so there's no point in even askin' about it."

"You talk to the bastard. I sure as hell won't." Kenny was at the stage of drunkenness where he was capable only of slurring the same sentiments over and over again.

"When was the last time you saw Clete Byrnes, Sam?"

"Two days before he died."

"Where?"

"He stopped by our little cabin in back of the stage line."

"What did he talk about?"

"He said he was thinking of movin' on. Real fast-like."

"So he was nervous."

"Real nervous."

The sound of snoring cut through the conversation like a saw. Kenny's head rested on his chest. He was fast asleep.

"You shouldn't of shot his hand that way."

"Well, he shouldn't ought to have attacked me."

Sam shrugged. "He was scared, real scared. Clete was, I mean. I would've been, too. Two of them were dead. He had to know he was next in line. He said he was going to hide out somewhere."

"He give you any hint of where that was?"

"He didn't say. Don't blame him for that, either. You want to hide out, you don't want anybody else to know where you are."

"He mention who might be doing the killing?"

"No. And I asked him. I said that he must know something. But all he said was that I'd be surprised."

"When Sheriff Cain talked to you, did you tell him what Clete said?"

Irritation in the voice and eyes. "I didn't tell that sheriff jack shit. He's always treated me and Kenny like we was scum. I wouldn't help him if he was drowning."

"You telling me everything you know?"

Sullen now. "Yeah. But I probably shouldn't after what you done to Kenny's hand."

"Don't you want to find who killed Clete?"

"Yeah, and that's the only reason I'm talkin' to you."

"You have any opinion about who it was?"

"Hell, yes, I do. Ned Lenihan. And everybody knows it. He knew them three boys all their lives. They used to hang around the stage line all the time they were growin' up. They worshipped him. They'd do whatever he asked them to. And that includes robbing a stage and splitting the money with him."

"You have any proof of that?"

"Don't need no more proof than the fact that he needs money bad for that farm of his. He don't want to look bad for his lady. She's another one I don't like. Kenny asked her to dance one Saturday night and she claimed he held her too tight and took some liberties. Everybody takes some liberties when they dance. A little feel here and there. Who does she think she is anyway?"

Kenny's snoring was louder now. Fargo decided he'd probably outstayed his welcome with the Raines boys. They weren't exactly the kind of company he cared to keep.

"Maybe you better put his head down on the table before he falls out of the chair," Fargo said as he stood up.

"Yeah," Sam snarled, "and maybe you shouldn't ought to have shot his gun hand."

The troubled feeling was still with Amy Peters as she stood near the counter where Ned Lenihan was helping a customer finish wrapping up a small box. In addition to selling tickets, overseeing the welfare of coaches and horses and paying salaries, Ned was also responsible for all the shipping. Cawthorne was getting big enough that this represented a significant portion of the small company's profits. Ned liked to joke that he had nightmares about never being able to speak any words but those of the cautions he gave people shipping things that might break. "You realize that the company can't take responsibility." He always said this in the self-mocking way that made her smile.

She hadn't intended to stop by today. She needed to get home. There was cooking, washing, sewing to do. But after her encounter with Tom Cain she felt a need to see Ned. The past few times she'd seen Cain there'd been a certain edge in his voice, almost a threat. And today's words—and maybe she was wrong, maybe she was hearing something that he really wasn't saying—today's words seemed to carry a warning of some kind.

"Your quilt'll be fine, Mrs. Swanson," Ned said to the older lady who had reached into the pocket of her long skirt to dig out her coins. "Now that we've got the string tightened up and everything."

Her clawlike right hand showed why she hadn't been able to wrap the package properly. Arthritis. The knuckles swollen, the fingers twisted. "You sure do take care of people nice, Ned. That's why everybody likes you."

"And here I thought they liked me because of my good looks."

A sweet smile on Mrs. Swanson's face. "And you make me laugh."

When the transaction was done, the old lady, picking her way with her cane, looked up and saw Amy standing there. "I sure wouldn't let him get away, Amy. He's the best man in this whole town."

"You don't have to worry about that, Mrs. Swanson."

She went on out, leaving them alone in the small office. Schedules and promotional material cluttered the walls in front of the counter. Behind were two desks and five filing cabinets. The back door led to the corral and barn where the vehicles were worked on.

"Well, you're looking more beautiful than ever, Amy."

"A touch of the blarney in all Irishmen, as my aunt Mae used to say."

"Well, remembering her husband, she married a man with more than a touch of it."

They often joked about Amy's uncle Dick. He was a decent man but a poor one. This didn't stop him from always giving other poor people advice on how they could become wealthy. People always told him that if his advice was good he should take it himself.

Then Ned said, "Something wrong, Amy?" Studying her face now.

She put her hand out and he took it. She knew she was making a fool of herself but she couldn't help it. She needed to reassure herself that everything in her little world was all right, safe. That Ned and she would finally get married and live out their lives together.

"I just got sentimental I guess, is all." What she wanted to tell him was how much she feared for him. The whispers she was hearing. Her continuing distrust of Tom Cain.

He leaned across the counter and she met him halfway. They kissed.

"Well, stop in any time you get sentimental, Mrs. Peters. I'll be happy to oblige you."

Door opened. Bell above it rang. She felt color in her cheeks. Had Mrs. Riley, a professional gossip, seen them kissing? Apparently not, because Mrs. Riley's scowl wasn't nearly as deep as usual.

"Hope you're having a good day, Mrs. Riley," Amy said.

"I've had better ones," Mrs. Riley said.

She was always such good company, Amy thought. If you liked complainers.

Mrs. Riley was one of those tall women who got too close to you when you talked so that you had to look up to her. She also tended to shout rather than simply speak. Apparently she had only two dresses she was willing to wear in public. A dark blue one and a black one. Shoulders and cuffs were white lace and they were belted in the middle. Today she wore the black one.

She set a small, carefully wrapped package on the counter.

"Now, Ned, I'm not necessarily blaming you for this but the last time I gave you a package to send, the wrapping string came loose. I would prefer that not happen this time."

Even from the opposite end of the counter Amy could see that the white string around the box was already loose.

"I'll be sure to take care of that for you, Mrs. Riley."

Mrs. Riley glanced at Amy. "I consider you a very lucky woman to be engaged to Ned here, Amy. And I defend him every chance I get. As far as I know he didn't have anything to do with that robbery or these terrible killings."

Amy felt her face burn. Anger and embarrassment. "Well, that's very nice of you, Mrs. Riley." Wanting to spare Ned any further talk of the matter.

But Mrs. Riley wasn't finished. "I know you need money for that farm of yours you should've given up a long time ago. If you had, Ned, people wouldn't be so suspicious of you. That's one thing. And as for the killings—I always say that Ned is a sweet little man. Some of my friends always wondered why Amy here didn't take up with Sheriff Cain. He's so handsome and strong and—well, manly—but I always say that Ned is a comfort. And maybe that's what Amy needs at this time in her life."

"That's so sweet of you, Mrs. Riley," Amy said, now more amused than angry. "And when people speak up against you, I'm always the first to say that just because she gossips and tells lies doesn't mean that deep down she isn't a very pleasant woman."

Now it was Mrs. Riley's face that flushed red. The blue gaze scorched Amy's face. "I see. A decent woman offers her support to a man the whole town thinks set up that robbery and killed those three poor boys and you think it's all right to mock her? Are you going to let her insult me this way, Ned?"

"Well, if she hadn't, Mrs. Riley, I would have." Ned picked up her small box. "The string is already loose. Just as it was on the last box. But this time I'm going to do you the favor of retying it for you."

She snatched the box from his hands. "I'll mail it. Ralph at the post office would never let anybody mock me."

Lenihan's Irish eyes twinkled with malice. "Maybe you don't know what he says about you after you've gone."

She stormed to the door. "Now I know that what people say about you is true. And I hope they hang you."

She slammed the door so hard the glass shivered.

Amy took Ned's hands in hers. "I shouldn't have said anything. I just couldn't help it. That old crone."

"Don't worry about it. Ralph called her out a couple of years ago just the way you did. That's why she started using the stage." He smiled. "I feel sorry for Ralph."

Amy laughed. "She's quite a woman, isn't she?"

But for all the humor of the moment, Mrs. Riley's words worried Amy. The town was beginning to see Ned as the number one suspect. In a situation as volatile as this one, that was a frightening realization.

9

The woman who approached Fargo was the handsome blond sister of the dead man he'd discovered. Karen Byrnes had changed into a ruffled white blouse and black skirt. A red woolen shawl over her shoulders flattered her blue eyes and rose-colored lips. She carried a large cloth purse over one arm.

Fargo had just left the Gold Mine when she waved to him and hurried to meet him. After sitting with the Raines brothers he welcomed contact with a gentler soul. The way she filled out her blouse made talking to her even more enticing.

With the clatter and clutter of wagons and buggies behind her, she reached him slightly out of breath. "I've been looking for you for the past half hour, Mr. Fargo."

"You could always call me Skye."

"Skye, then. Thank you."

The ivory skin was tainted only around the eyes. She'd been crying.

"You probably won't like what I have to say."

"I doubt that but let's hear it first and see."

She touched his arm with careful fingers. He liked that. "I've been playing detective. I promise I won't do it again. But I thought of a woman named Ingrid Haller. Her son was one of the three boys killed. She told me about a man named Rex who saw somebody talking to the boys just before the first one was killed."

"Did he say who?"

"No. Not to her anyway. I was wondering if you and I—"

He put a hand on her shoulder. "I work alone. I'm not

even taking Tom Cain along with me. But I appreciate your offer."

Before he knew quite what she was doing, she slid her arm through his and began walking them down the street. A pair of lovers out for a stroll. That was the mood she was obviously trying to set. A smart young woman able to put her grief aside to get what she wanted. In order to find the man or men who'd murdered her brother.

"Rex is a recluse. For most people he won't even come to the door. And he has a dog."

"This seems to be the town for guard dogs."

"Do you know Helen Hardesty?"

"Matter of fact I do."

"Rex's wolfhound is the father of Helen's wolfhound."

"Can't wait to meet him. Helen almost sicced hers on me."

"She's a feisty lady."

"I noticed that."

"Anyway, Rex won't talk to you. You'll need me along."

"He has an eye for beauty, then."

"Why, thank you. But no, that isn't it at all. I knew him growing up before he was a recluse. He was an usher at our church and I sang in the children's choir. Once a week I bake bread for him and bring it over."

"Makes sense. But just because he'll let you in—us in—doesn't mean he'll tell us anything."

"I think he can be persuaded." She tapped her purse. "I'm bringing him this week's bread. And not just one loaf but two."

"A very enterprising young woman."

"Well, if I don't keep busy, I'll lose my mind. Thinking about Clete—" She choked back tears.

Holding her arm closer to his side, he said, "Then let's go see Rex."

Eyes.

A few weeks ago when Ned Lenihan walked down a Cawthorne street everybody had a smile and a hello for him. Made sense. Lenihan was generally a mild and friendly man to just about everybody. From helping people build their barns to giving money to those in need, Lenihan was known to care deeply about the welfare of other folks.

A few weeks ago that had all changed. The secret strongbox filled with money. The robbery. The murder of the Englishman and driver. The murders of the three boys. And now it was all changed and likely changed forever.

Eyes.

As he walked to the sheriff's office he stared into the faces of old friends and found strangers. Found in those eyes distrust and contempt. Found in those eyes anger and a certainty that he had been involved in all of it.

The gazes lashed him. Even the few who spoke to him only grunted, as if they were embarrassed to even acknowledge his existence. What was the word in the Bible? Pariah. Yes, that's what he'd become. A pariah to his own town.

When he finally reached the sheriff's office, he noticed that people stopped in their tracks to watch him. Did they think he was going in there to confess? Wouldn't that be a good show for them all?

He opened the door and pushed in.

Pete Rule sat behind the small desk to the right of Tom Cain's. Lenihan was both disappointed and relieved. Disappointed that he wouldn't have his confrontation with Cain and relieved that the confrontation wouldn't happen. His feelings were all crazy these days.

Rule had been writing on a large pad of paper. His eyes showed surprise when he saw who it was. "Morning, Ned."

"Cain not around, Pete?"

"Over to the courthouse."

"Oh." Lenihan stood there looking around as if he'd never seen the sheriff's office before.

"Something I can do for you, Ned?"

Lenihan appreciated Rule's tone. The two had never been close friends but they'd always been friendly. Rule had had to suffer Cain's arrogance the way everybody else in town had and Lenihan often found himself feeling sorry for the deputy.

"Well, I was going to talk to Cain."

"Maybe something I can help you with?" Rule dropped the pencil he'd been using and leaned back in his chair. "You all right, Ned? You look pale."

"I feel pale."

"Why don't you sit down in that chair there? How about some coffee?"

"Coffee would be good." Lenihan's voice was faint and he felt dizzy. He'd begun to sweat. He inched his way to the chair and sat down while Rule got him coffee.

"Here you go, Ned. You sure you're all right?"

Lenihan took a deep breath as he accepted the tin cup of coffee. "It's getting to me, Pete."

"What is?" Rule said as he took his place behind his desk again.

"You know what I'm talking about. You know damned well what I'm talking about."

Rule nodded. "It'll blow over, Ned. You know how people are. They reach for the easiest answer. And for some reason right now you're the easiest answer."

"But it's the wrong answer."

"I know that and I tell everybody that."

"The way I figure it, Cain's behind this. He's the one stirring this up."

"Well—"

"You know it's true."

"How's the coffee?"

"C'mon, Pete. Help me. You know Cain's behind this."

"It isn't just Cain, Ned. It's everybody. You work there. You're in charge of things. It's logical in one way—even if it's wrong."

"Is it logical that I killed those three boys—even if I was involved in the robbery, do you really think I could kill those three boys?"

"It isn't logical to me. But people start talking and"—he leaned forward on his elbows—"you need to tell me everything you know, Ned."

Exasperation in his voice, Lenihan said, "You've known

me for twenty years. I recommended you for the job when Cain first came here before I knew what he was like. You've known Amy and her family longer than I have. And you've still got doubts about me, Pete?"

"I'm just being a deputy, Ned. That's all. If you tell me you didn't have anything to do with it, I'll believe you."

"I didn't have anything to do with it."

"All right. I'm throwing in with you. I'm going to bring it up with Cain the next time I see him. He should be back here in a while."

Lenihan paused. "You ever consider the possibility that Cain is behind all this?"

"Aw, c'mon now, Ned. Just because you didn't have anything to do with it doesn't mean that Cain did."

"He's still after Amy."

"He gave that up."

"That's what he says. But think about it. With me out of the way he might still think he has a chance with her. He's not the kind of man who gets turned down very often. And it embarrassed him. A lot of people sort of laughed about it and he knew that. Maybe this is his chance to get up a lot of money and take another crack at Amy. He'd have a clear field if I was out of the way."

Rule went over and poured himself more coffee. He tipped the pot in Lenihan's direction but Lenihan shook his head. Rule came back and perched himself on the edge of the desk. "You're wasting your time thinking about that, Ned. And I'm saying that as your friend."

The door opened and Tom Cain walked in. His eyes reflected his surprise at seeing Lenihan sitting across from Rule.

"You stop by to confess, did you, Ned?" The rueful, condescending tone Lenihan was used to hearing.

"You might be the killer yourself, Cain."

"That's just like a guilty man, isn't it, Pete? Trying to put the blame on somebody else. We see that a lot, don't we?"

"We were just having a talk, Tom." Rule's eyes met Lenihan's. "And he wasn't confessing to anything. He's just worried that so many people think he's the man we're looking for."

Lenihan was already on his feet. "I want you to stop spreading rumors about me."

"And what makes you think I'm doing that?" He brushed past Lenihan, making sure he nudged him on the way over to his own desk. He took off his Stetson, hung it on the hat rack and then seated himself. "The people in this town aren't stupid, Lenihan. They know you need money and they know you knew all about the money in the strongbox. Doesn't take much to figure out who might be behind it."

"How about you, like I said? Or the Raines brothers?"

"You accusing them, too, are you, Lenihan?" Cain's smug manner only infuriated Lenihan all the more. "Pretty soon you'll start accusing everybody who passes you on the street."

"Easy, Tom. There's no solid evidence against him. There's just a lot of suspicion." Rule's voice was sympathetic and obviously irritated the lawman.

"You throwing in with him, are you, Pete? Seems to me you need to be a little more objective when it comes to suspects."

"How about you, Cain?" Lenihan said. "How objective are you? You've hated me ever since you started chasing Amy around. You couldn't stand the thought that she turned you down. You've been waiting for a chance to bring me down ever since."

"If I wanted to bring you down, Lenihan, it wouldn't take much. I'm older than you and not in the peak of condition but I'll be happy to fight you with fists or guns anytime you name it."

Lenihan's mind blanked. Some unconscious force took over him. He found himself diving through the air straight across Cain's desk, smashing into the startled lawman and knocking him out of his chair. He didn't stop there. Before Rule could reach him, Lenihan struck Cain in the face twice. Despite the small size of his fists, he managed to bloody the lawman's mouth and to give him a small cut above the left eye.

Rule shouted, "You're just making it worse, Ned!" He got his arms around Ned's shoulders and jerked the small man to his feet. Then he shoved him back several feet.

By now Cain was struggling to his feet. Shouting curses, touching the blood on his lips in disbelief. His eyes showed the insanity they often did when he was in any kind of altercation. As his hand dropped to his six-shooter, Rule shouted, "No, Tom!"

And to make sure Cain didn't draw and fire, Rule lodged himself in front of his boss. "You need to simmer down and so does Ned."

"Who're you working for, Pete?" Cain shouted. "Me or Lenihan?"

"For you, Tom. But I sure as hell don't want to see anybody get killed over this."

"And what if he's the one who killed those boys? Do you want to see him die then, do you?"

"I don't believe he's the one, Tom. But if he is, then I'll have to see what I think then."

"You get out of here, Lenihan," Cain bellered. "Right now you're hiding behind Pete. But if he wasn't here you'd be dead, you understand?"

Rule faced Lenihan. Seeing that Lenihan was about to say something—still looking belligerent—he pushed him toward the door and said, "Out and out now, Ned. Right now!"

Lenihan, shaking his head, staring down at his bruised knuckles, looked up and scowled at Cain. And then, still shaking his head, left the sheriff's office.

"What the hell's that for?" Sam Raines said.

"I'd say that isn't any of your business."

"Well, since I'm the one that cleaned up all your puke a little while ago, I'd say it sure is my business."

"Well, I've been known to clean up your puke when I need to." Which was true. Sam did his own share of alcohol vomiting, too.

The shack behind the stage line had once been used for drivers to sleep in. It contained two cots, a potbelly stove, wooden flooring and no windows. One driver had remarked that it was one step up from a prison cell. No meals were made or eaten here. The Raines brothers had taken it over after the stage line got a reduced room rate from the worst hotel in Cawthorne for its drivers. At least the hotel rooms had windows and didn't have the suffocating smell of men to whom bathing was often considered an offense.

After the confrontation with Fargo earlier, Sam had guided his brother back to the cabin where he had promptly sprayed chunky vomit all over the floor. Sam had stashed Kenny against a tree and then proceeded to swamp up the disgusting awful puke. He'd dragged Kenny inside and pitched him on his cot. And then he'd taken some sleep himself.

When he woke up he saw Kenny sitting on the edge of his cot holding his Winchester. Couple of things wrong here. Kenny wasn't exactly a master with a rifle. Even when they'd been little boys hunting, Sam had been the one with the eye and the trigger finger. The second thing wrong was that Kenny's shooting hand was wrapped in a bandage. And Sam could tell that it still hurt him because just in the past minute or two Kenny had winced three times. So what the hell was he doing with the Winchester?

"I'm gonna take care of Fargo."

"You mean Fargo's gonna take care of you."

"You hate him, too."

"I hate him, too, but that don't mean I want to tangle with him. And anyway, he'll be gone soon enough. I heard he's leavin' tomorrow."

"Look at this, you son of a bitch." Kenny held up his wrapped hand dramatically. "I won't never be able to shoot right again."

"Well, truth be told, Kenny, you know what the old man said. He said neither of us was worth a whit as fast draws."

"I killed two men, didn't I?"

"I just want to relax. I drank a lot myself and I'm sick as hell."

"I said I killed two men, didn't I?"

"You killed them from behind. That ain't the same thing."

"But I killed them. There're a lot of men who wouldn't kill another man no matter what."

"So you're going to kill Fargo from the back?"

"No, brother, *you're* gonna shoot Fargo from the back."

Sam spat on the floor. "The hell I am."

"The hell you ain't. Unless you want me to tell people what that whore said about you that night in Denver."

"She was just pissed because I cheated her out of her money."

"She said you didn't measure up."

"Yeah, well you can't find any other whore I ever been with who said that. I do all right for myself and you can bet on it."

"So you don't mind if I talk that around?"

A long, hurt silence. Sometimes it seemed to Sam that Kenny wasn't his real brother at all. He could get as snake-mean with his own blood as he could a stranger. Many was the time Sam thought of leaving Cawthorne and Kenny behind. But when he started to think it through he always decided against it because where would he go? He wasn't the sort who made friends fast. He didn't have any money, he didn't have Kenny's way of intimidating people and he had to face it—he got lonesome pretty easy.

"I never shot nobody in the back."

"You never shot nobody period."

"Well, that's a hell of a way to start, isn't it? Shootin' somebody in the back?"

"Look at this, Sam. Look at what he done to my hand." Kenny waved his hand around as if it was on display. "Don't you have no family pride? You know what our pa would say if he was alive?"

Sam sighed. "Yeah, I know what he'd say. He'd say to kill him any way you had to."

"That's right. And you know it."

"You started it though, Kenny—you rushed him and—"

"You're just makin' excuses and you know it."

Sam sighed again. It was hard to deny his brother when

the old man was brought into the argument. Sam had always felt that he'd let the old man down most of the time. And Kenny was sure right about this one. The old man would have raised holy hell if he'd known that Sam wouldn't avenge the family honor and kill Fargo.

"All right, Kenny," Sam said, "I don't want to do it but I guess I will."

10

Karen Byrnes had been right about Rex Connor's wolf-hound. It was an older version of Helen Hardesty's animal. And not one iota friendlier. It greeted them with snarls and growls as they reached the property where a tumbledown cabin sat in a grove of jack pines. An ancient mule was tethered to a clothesline pole. Red long johns flapped in the wind.

The door to the cabin opened an inch or two. A disembodied voice said, "You're welcome here, Karen, but not the man."

"He's helping me, Rex. We're trying to find out who killed my brother."

"I can't help you there. Now you both git."

The door slammed.

"He's afraid."

"Of what?"

"I'm not sure. Ever since the killings started."

"Afraid somebody'll come after him?"

"That's what I thought. But I wonder."

A chill wind smelling of pine brought a foretaste of winter as they stood staring at the cabin door.

"I talked to Ingrid this morning, Rex. She said you saw somebody talking to my brother and the other two one night. It would help us a lot if you'd tell us who you saw."

"You need to leave, Karen."

"You must be out of bread, Rex."

"I don't care about bread. Now you go along and take that big man with you."

The wolfhound growled, as if to second its master's command.

"Well, I don't know what to do with this bread. I have two loaves here and one of them is cinnamon."

A long pause. "Cinnamon?"

"Yes. I know that's your favorite."

"Who's the man?"

"His name's Skye Fargo. He's helping me like I said. We really need to talk to you, Rex."

"I don't want to get nobody in trouble."

"You read the Bible, Rex. And you know what the Bible says about telling the truth."

Another long pause. "Are they both cinnamon, did you say?"

"One of them's cinnamon. But if you'll talk I'll make you another loaf of it next time, too."

The door creaked open. A short man with a long white beard dressed in a green flannel shirt, grimy jeans and boots that laced up to his knees emerged. The first thing he did was spit out a stream of chaw and the second thing he did was hitch up his britches. He had only one suspender.

"You sit right there, King. If that feller makes a move, you get ready."

The wolfhound must have understood the tone if not the exact meaning of the words. Its magnificent head swept around to Rex Connor, as if it had understood everything.

"I told Ingrid not to say nothing."

"Her son's dead, Rex. My brother's dead. We need help."

"What's this Fargo got to do with it?"

"He's helping Tom Cain."

"Tom Cain." He spat more tobacco. "I wouldn't trust Tom Cain if my life depended on it."

"Maybe your life doesn't, but since we haven't caught the killer yet maybe somebody's does."

Fargo realized that this could go on a long time. He said, "If you know something you need to tell us. If somebody else gets killed you might be partly responsible. We don't have much time. So I'd appreciate it if you'd let us know who you saw with the three boys that night."

"What if I said I didn't recognize him?"

"Then I'd say you're a liar."

"Skye!" Karen said. "Don't insult him!"

But the Trailsman was tired of the conversation. He took two steps forward, knowing he would set the dog off.

"One more step and he'll jump you, Fargo," Connor said.

"Then he'll have to jump me."

Fargo felt Karen's hand clutching his shirt. "Skye, it's not worth it."

"Yes, it is."

Fargo raised his right leg and started to take a step. His eyes were fixed on Connor's face. He hoped the old buzzard would relent. He was betting on it.

The wolfhound stood up. Arched its body.

Fargo began to put his foot to the ground, to take the final step.

"Cinnamon, you say?" Connor said. "That's the only reason I'll do it. Not because I'm afraid of this here gunfighter."

Fargo swallowed his smile. Every man wanted to save face. No man wanted to be seen backing down. Not even this old coot. He did it himself. "Good thing you agreed to it. The dog would've made a mess of me but I would've pumped you full of lead before he killed me."

"Oh, God," Karen Byrnes said, "is it any wonder I hate men?"

When Amy heard about the fight between Ned and Tom Cain, she rushed from the general store and began running to the stagecoach office. The two men who had taken great delight in telling her about it came out on the stoop in front of the store and clucked their disapproval of both Amy and Ned Lenihan. They were of the mind that Lenihan had killed the three boys to keep them from revealing his part in the robbery.

Amy stumbled twice, once nearly falling to the ground,

saved only by a man who reached down and brought her to her feet. But not even that slowed her. She wanted to hold Ned. Keep him safe. Tom Cain had been an enemy before. Now he could afford to openly pursue Ned.

She was startled to see Ned at the counter filling out a form. As if nothing had happened. When he raised his head she saw a small bruise on his right cheek. Otherwise he looked fine.

There were no customers so she didn't worry about pushing through the wooden gate and going to him. She lifted the pencil from his hand and took him in her arms.

She said nothing, just held him. She could feel his heart beat. The way it raced, she knew that he was afraid too. What he'd done had been reckless. She didn't blame him. Cain had pushed him far too long. His rage must have been overwhelming. By rights he would not stand a chance against Cain. But he'd likely snapped and pounced on Cain before the lawman knew what was happening. In other circumstances she would have been happy for Ned. But not now. Not when so many people in town thought he was guilty. Not now when Cain had been waiting for some excuse to move on Ned.

She found herself kissing him passionately. She found herself weeping, her tears dampening the faces of both of them.

As he tore off pieces of cinnamon bread and stuffed them into his mouth, Rex Connor managed to salt his white beard with bits of bread and sprays of his own spittle. It wasn't a pretty sight, especially since he was more concentrated on his eating than answering Fargo's question.

Standing in the thinning sunlight outside Rex's cabin, Fargo said, "So you saw a man talking to the three boys that night?"

Rex nodded. His mouth was too full to speak.

"And you recognized him?"

Another nod.

"But you're afraid you'll get him in trouble if you tell us who you saw?"

Rex gulped down some bread and said, "That's right."

"What if he was the killer?" Fargo said. He was tired of taking his time with this old fart. If Karen hadn't been here he would have grabbed him and shaken the truth out of him. "You want to protect a killer?"

"He ain't no killer."

"You're sure of that?"

Instead of answering, Rex tore off another piece of bread with his grimy hands. "I've known this feller a long, long time. I guess I'd know if he was a killer or not, wouldn't I?"

"People surprise you sometimes."

"Not this feller. He don't surprise me."

"Rex, please, please tell us who you saw," Karen said. "We won't hurt him. We'll just talk to him."

"And she baked you that bread," Fargo said, feeling ridiculous. What the hell was he doing, talking about bread when he should have been grabbing this bastard and choking the answer out of him? He steadied himself. "And from the looks of your beard, you seem to be enjoying it."

"I'll just get him in trouble and he's got trouble enough with his farm."

As soon as he said it, Rex looked shocked, as if somebody else might have said it. But it had popped out and now, even without naming the man, both Fargo and Karen knew who he was talking about.

"You're saying it was Lenihan."

"That ain't what I said, Fargo."

"Maybe not. But it's what you meant."

"Ned," Karen said, as if she couldn't believe it. "Ned Lenihan."

"See, just what I told ya," Rex said, chawing around a piece of bread. "Now you've got him tried and convicted and you don't even know what he was doin' with them boys."

"You saw him only that one time?"

"Yep. Only that one time, Fargo. And you're makin' way too much of it."

"But you don't have any doubt who you saw."

"Nope. None at all."

Fargo watched Karen's face grow tight with concern. On the one hand, Lenihan was the name most often heard when people talked about the chief suspect. On the other hand, Lenihan's few defenders were positive that he was innocent.

There was only one way to find out.

"Thanks, Rex."

"You're gonna go after him, ain't you, Fargo?"

"I'm going to find out why he was talking to those boys. That's all."

Rex looked genuinely sorry. "He's a good man. I shouldn't a said nothing."

"It's all right, Rex," Karen said. "You did the right thing."

"Make trouble for an innocent man?" Rex scoffed. "You call that doing the right thing?"

But he went right on eating.

The son's name was George Lenihan. He was an inch or two taller than his father but was stamped with the same small, fine Irish facial features and slight if wiry body. He wore a black seaman's sweater, in deference to the increasingly chilly day, and a pair of jeans. He stood in front of a white barn and watched Fargo approach. He'd been working and had a pitchfork in his hand.

Fargo dismounted, walked toward him. He'd gotten the name and some background on the son from Karen. The son had lived here since his wife left him two years ago. They'd been childless, the wife suffering three miscarriages in as many years. It was Karen's impression that this had contributed to the wife's leaving.

Fargo noted wryly that no angry dogs had yet put in an appearance.

"Afternoon," Fargo said amiably.

"Who the hell're you?"

"Name's Fargo."

"Oh. My pa told me about you. You're the one who works for Tom Cain."

"Not 'for.' 'With.' I'm just lending him a hand. But I don't take orders from him if that's what you've got in mind."

"Right now I'm wondering what *you've* got in mind."

"I was wondering if you'd let me look around the farm."

Narrow eyes grew narrower. Knuckles whitened on the pitchfork. "For what reason?"

"You want a nice little lie or the truth?"

"The truth."

"A good share of Cawthorne thinks your father had something to do with the robbery and the killings of those three men."

"They were boys. Not men. Hell-raisers. And anybody who thinks my pa had anything to do with any of it is wrong."

"Then you won't mind if I look around?"

"On whose orders?"

"Mine."

"Not Cain's?"

"He doesn't even know I'm here."

George Lenihan surveyed the farm outbuildings and the small house. "You won't find anything."

"I hope I won't."

The son looked even more like the father when concern shadowed his face. "He's a good man. I worry about him. People will believe anything sometimes. That's why I stay on the farm here. I've had enough of people to last me a lifetime."

Fargo wondered how much George's dislike of people came from the woman who'd left him.

"I want to believe your father, George."

"Why?"

"Maybe because I'm like you. I believe that people will believe anything if they hear it often enough. You start accusing somebody of something and pretty soon everybody around begins to claim it's true."

"That's what's happening to my pa."

"Well, then let me look around and we'll prove that they're wrong."

The son shrugged. "There's a collie roaming around here. She's very friendly. She won't give you any trouble."

"A friendly dog," Fargo said. "Imagine that."

"Where do you want to start?"

"In the house."

"Pa and I ain't exactly housekeepers."

"I'll probably get over the shock."

"This pisses me off."

"Figured it would. But maybe it'll help your father in the long run."

"Yeah, sure it will."

The wood-framed house was pretty orderly considering there was no woman living in it. The furniture was old, most likely bought by Lenihan's wife, running to flowered curtains, doily-covered furniture and numerous framed religious paintings on the wall. The place hadn't been dusted in a long time and the air was sour with cooking smells. Fargo spent most of his time going through the rolltop desk and six wooden boxes that were stuffed with everything from pans that had been burned through to old clothes that could no longer be patched up. He found nothing.

The collie was waiting for him at the back door. She was a handsome golden girl. Fargo had no doubt that she could rip open a human body anytime she chose to but he enjoyed the fact that when he bent down she let him pet her. She had restored his faith in the canine world.

George Lenihan had gone back to his haying near the fence running in back of the barn. From what Fargo could see, the crops were typical for this part of Colorado—onions, sugar beets, vegetables.

He headed downslope to the barn, the affable collie following him. The haymow door was open, allowing light into the shadowy interior. Smells of hay, horse manure, damp earth greeted him. A buggy stood to one side of the barn while farming tools lined the opposite wall. There were four stalls for horses and a makeshift bench for carpentry. Saws, hammers, a keg of nails surrounded butt ends of lumber that had been sawn.

As with the house, he had no idea what he was looking

for, just some vague notion that he needed to find something physical to connect Ned Lenihan with the robbery.

The collie stayed with him. During his search, he took several opportunities to pet her. She was a good companion. Beautiful face and such clean gold and white fur.

The first half hour turned up nothing more interesting than a few stacks of yellowed magazines, a small box of toys that had probably been George's, a few old saddles. The only interesting items were in a box—equipment for gold mining, a sluice box, pans, a pair of pickaxes. Fargo wondered if Ned had gotten caught up in the gold rush and then the silver rush that had brought so many people to the Territory. Everybody who could wield a shovel had gone crazy for sudden riches— and were still doing so. But Lenihan struck Fargo as sensible. He might have spent a few foolish weeks or months in the mountains but he couldn't see Lenihan spending any more time than that.

Then he noticed that the box with mining equipment in it wobbled slightly. It was sitting on something that made it tilt. He lifted it up and saw that there was fresh earth underneath it. Somebody had dug a hole and buried something in it.

Fargo got down on his haunches. The collie was right next to him. He could smell her hot breath. She was as interested in the loose earth as he was. He started digging with his hands. His first surprise was how shallow the hole was. His second surprise was what it contained.

He got to his feet again. The thing in his hand dripped fresh dirt. He hadn't bothered to brush it off. He walked out of the barn and into the mountain sunlight. He wasn't sure what to think. If a man was in a hurry he wouldn't have had time to bury it deep. But why on his own property would he be in a hurry? On the other hand, being that it *was* his own property, he probably wouldn't have to care about it being buried deep. Especially since it was in the barn. Especially since it was covered up by a box.

Then there was another question. Why would a man keep this at all? What good would it do him?

He didn't like any of this. Maybe he was somehow sorry for Ned Lenihan and coming up with all these questions just to exonerate him. Maybe it was just as simple as it looked. He'd lifted up the box and found the fresh earth and dug it up and found the thing. The thing that would lead any reasonable detective, Pinkerton or not, to conclude that Ned Lenihan had been involved in the robbery for sure and very possibly in the murders.

He walked over to the fence. The collie trotted alongside him. He cupped a hand to his mouth and yelled for George Lenihan. Lenihan stopped his haying, planted his pitchfork in the earth and came over.

Long before he reached the fence, Lenihan saw what Fargo was holding. When he reached the Trailsman, he said, "What's that?"

But he knew what it was. And he knew what it meant, too.

Fargo held it up. "It's got the name of the bank stenciled right on it." The bag was the size of a regular satchel. It had a lock attached to a leather section at the top. The lock had been shot off.

"Where'd you find it?"

"You know what it is and you know where I found it."

"My pa didn't put that there."

"Somebody did."

George Lenihan's arms came across the fence and tried to grab Fargo's throat. "You sonofabitch! You brought that with you and then claimed to have found it in the barn!"

Fargo might have felt sorry for him if the man's hands weren't struggling to strangle him. Fargo hit him hard with the heavy bag, knocking him off-balance, sending him stumbling backward and finally falling to the ground on his ass.

"He didn't do it! My pa didn't do it!"

The beautiful collie started barking sharply, as if in sympathy.

Fargo dropped the bag and went over and offered George Lenihan his hand. Lenihan slapped it away. "You put it there. You had it on your horse when you came in. You put it there when I was out haying."

"You know better than that."

"Do I? This whole town has turned against him." He put a palm flat against the grassy soil and started the process of pushing himself to his feet. "Cain sent you here to do this. And now you'll take my pa in, won't you?"

"I won't have any choice. I found this in his barn."

Lenihan's shoulders slumped in defeat. "Don't you see what's going on here, Fargo? All right, say you didn't do it. But don't you see that somebody else planted it? Somebody who wants to ruin my pa."

"Who would that be?"

"Who do you think? Who's been chasing after Amy all these years?"

"Cain says he's given up on her."

"Cain says, Cain says. Cain says a lot of things and half of them are damned lies. Think about it. He sets up the robbery, he gets all the money after he kills the three boys and now he gets to destroy my father. Maybe he can't have Amy but he can get the satisfaction of seeing my father hang."

"Look," Fargo said. "I'll check out everything you say. Everything. I promise. And if I think this has been planted here that's what I'll tell Cain. And if I think it's been planted and I suspect it's Cain, I'll go after him."

"What can you do up against Cain? He runs this town."

"But he doesn't run me."

Lenihan choked back a sob. "You don't know my pa. He's the kindest man I've ever known. And the people in town know that too. But they've let all this gossip make them crazy. They're just layin' for him. And it scares me." He paused, stared at the bank bag. "Is there any way—"

"You know I can't do that. I have to take this in and talk to your father. And most likely take him to jail."

"He needs to be safe, Fargo. You've got to promise me that. That he'll be safe."

"I'll make sure of that."

The collie responded to Lenihan's sadness by rubbing against his leg and making a sort of whimpering sound. She was a good dog in all respects.

"I need to get back now."

The conversation finished, Fargo turned and cut through a small collection of chickens.

He'd gone only a few steps when Lenihan called, "Stop right there, Fargo. I've got a gun on you. I want you to drop that bag and then get on your horse and ride out."

"You going to shoot me?"

"If I have to."

"Then I guess you'll have to."

"I'm not fooling."

"Neither am I."

Fargo began slowly moving to his big Ovaro.

"Fargo. Stop."

But Fargo kept moving. By now he was sure the kid wouldn't shoot. He turned when he reached the stallion. Lenihan looked pathetic. He had a useless gun in his hand and what appeared to be tears in his eyes.

Lenihan didn't say anything and neither did Fargo. There was nothing to say.

11

The bank bag, still showing traces of the dirt in which it had been buried, lay on the desk of Sheriff Tom Cain. He raised his pleased gaze to meet Fargo's eyes.

"In Lenihan's barn, you say?" Cain said.

"You heard me. No need to gloat."

"You don't sound happy."

"It strikes me as strange that he'd bury it in such an obvious way," Fargo said.

Standing next to him, Pete Rule said, "I agree. Ned's a smart man."

"He's also a good friend of yours, Pete. You and Fargo here just don't want to admit he's guilty."

Cain had been enjoying one of his smelliest cigars. Late afternoon sunlight was turned blue by the smoke. There was also the faint aroma of whiskey on the air. Cain had been known to take a drink during duty hours.

Cain took his feet down from his desk finally and sat up straight. "Since I make the decisions in this town—I'm the duly appointed law here as some people seem to be forgetting these days—I'm going to go arrest him myself."

"I found the bag. Let me go make the arrest."

"I don't remember appointing you as a deputy."

"Then give me a badge."

"And why should I do that, Skye?"

"Because you'll take too much pleasure in arresting him for one thing. And for another, you won't give him a chance to explain himself."

"In other words, you'll let him come up with some story

about the bank bag being planted there. And how about the story old Rex told you? That he saw Lenihan talking to the three boys down by the creek? You don't believe that, either?"

"I believe it but I'd like to hear Lenihan's side of it."

"You should give him a chance to talk anyway," Rule said.

"Why don't you go arrest him, Pete?" Amusement played in Cain's voice.

"Well, I—"

Cain stood up. "Well, look at this. Fargo finds the bank bag and hears a man swear that he saw Lenihan talking to the boys and he still doesn't think Lenihan's the one we're looking for. And poor Pete here's so much a friend of Lenihan's that he won't do his sworn duty and go arrest him."

"I'm still thinking you might be behind all this, Tom," Fargo said. "You set up the robbery and you killed those boys."

"Now, Fargo—" Rule started to say.

"No, no, Pete. Let him talk. That's been on his mind the whole time. Fargo thinks I'm the one he's looking for."

"It's a possibility," Fargo said. "Same as Lenihan's a possibility."

"So I'm as much of a suspect as Lenihan? Did you find a bank bag in my house, did you?"

"No. But you could've planted that bag in Lenihan's barn."

"Trusting soul, aren't you?"

"I want the badge, Tom. Now."

"I have to admit, Skye, it would give me a whole lot of pleasure to arrest Lenihan and then march him down the street."

"I'll be bringing him in the back way."

One of Cain's theater smiles. "Why, you're no fun at all, Skye."

Then he dug up a badge for the Trailsman.

The Winchester barrel gleamed in the sunlight of the dying day. Out on the river a pair of fishermen in a rowboat waved to Sam and Kenny Raines. Kenny waved but Sam was too busy lining up his next shot. Five bottles sat on top of two boxes. He had fired three times and hit one bottle. Kenny had replaced it with a new one.

"I would've busted all five of them by now." The disgust in Kenny's voice was clear. "And if I had my gun hand back, Fargo'd be dead by now too."

"I'm doing what I can."

"You're one of those shots got to be right on top of a man before you can kill him. We ain't gonna have that chance with Fargo. You'll have to shoot him from a distance."

"Maybe we'll get lucky."

"That's bullshit and you know it. Now get back to practicing."

"I get sick of you pushing me around sometimes."

"Well, I get sick of you lettin' me down all the time. You could've killed him the other night at the Gold Mine and you didn't. I would've killed him for you."

Sam made a face and started sighting along the barrel again. He squinted, steadied himself, fired. Third bottle from the left exploded jagged pieces of glass into the winterlike chill coming off of the river.

He didn't wait for Kenny's response. He took another bottle down right after. This one exploded even more dramatically, in a dozen smaller pieces.

"How's that?" Sam snapped. "Maybe you'll shut your yap for a while."

"Try another one."

And by God if Sam didn't get that one, too.

"Maybe getting you mad is what you needed."

"Someday you might make me so mad I do somethin' about it."

"That'll be the day. Now you got two more to go."

"I was bein' serious, Kenny. Someday—"

"Yeah. There's always someday, ain't there, Sam? Now shoot."

Sam got one, missed another.

"Four out of five."

"I would've made it five out of five." He went right on. "We do it tonight. He stays at the Royale, he eats at the Trail's End and he spends time at the sheriff's office. All we need to do is trail him from one place to another. The easiest place will be the café because there's an alley across from it. He won't see us and by the time he's dead we'll be in the woods out here by the river."

"Maybe it won't be that easy."

"It'll be that easy if you can shoot straight."

"Somebody might see us."

"Not if we're fast."

"What if I miss?"

"If you miss," Kenny laughed, "I'll kill you."

Sam snickered. "You mean with your gun hand?"

"You think that's funny?"

"Looks like from now on I'll be the shooter in the family."

"Yeah," Kenny sneered. "Four out of five."

Ned Lenihan was wrapping a small box when Fargo walked in the door of the stage line. Lenihan's scowl told the Trailsman how welcome he was.

"You back to harass me some more?"

From behind his back Fargo took the bank bag. He threw it on the counter. He watched Lenihan's response carefully. The man's eyes registered what the bag was then showed concern. "Where'd you get this?"

But before Fargo could speak, the door opened and a boy of maybe ten came in breathlessly. He carried a flowered carpetbag that had been tied with twine into a tight package and addressed in big printed letters on the face of an envelope. "My ma wanted me to get this here and get right back. We're having beef tonight. My brother always eats on mine if I ain't there."

Lenihan obviously had trouble dealing with the kid. "Uh, I'll take care of this, Jimmy."

"She said I should get a receipt."

"I'll do that for her tomorrow."

"She was pretty sure, Mr. Lenihan. I'll get in trouble if I don't get that receipt."

"Dammit, Jimmy, tell your mother I'll take care of it tomorrow. Now get on home!"

Jimmy's face showed confusion. Fargo imagined that Ned Lenihan acting this way was probably unheard of, especially with kids. He was the gentle man everybody liked and admired. And here he was yelling at Jimmy. What was going on?

Lenihan sighed. "I'm sorry, Jimmy. I shouldn't have snapped at you like that."

Jimmy looked from Lenihan to Fargo and back again. The world of adults was a strange and unknowable place. First Mr. Lenihan blew up and now he was like his old familiar self, being nice.

"Just give me a minute, Jimmy. I'll fix you up with that receipt."

Jimmy smiled uncertainly.

As Lenihan took the box and filled out the receipt, he said, "I know your mother likes to make her beef with vegetables on it. She brought a whole pot of it to a church social once. One of the best meals I ever had." Fargo could tell the man was still fighting anxiety but he was trying to carry on as normally as possible. Lenihan finished the receipt and tore it off the pad and handed it to Jimmy.

"I hope your brother saves some beef for you."

"My ma said she'd watch my plate real careful. She wouldn't have sent me but my aunt's ailing and my ma wanted to send her this sweater. And besides, that carpetbag belongs to my aunt anyway."

"Well, you hurry on home, Jimmy. And say hello to your folks."

"Thanks, Mr. Lenihan."

When the door closed Lenihan said, "I shouldn't have snapped at him. He's a good boy. He comes from one of the nicest families in Cawthorne. They don't have any money but they're good folks."

Fargo wondered if Lenihan was putting on a show for

him. The good, humble man who ran the stage line. But somehow he doubted it. Not that that meant anything. In his experience Fargo had seen many decent men succumb to evil. Evil seemed to be in everybody. Containing it was the trick.

"Where'd you get this bag?" Lenihan asked.

"In your barn."

"That's a lie."

"Afraid it isn't."

"Somebody planted it there."

Fargo pushed the bag toward Lenihan. "There's a man who says he saw you talking to the three boys right before they started getting killed."

"I knew the boys from when they were little. Why wouldn't I be talking to them?"

"One night down by the creek. Sounded like a secret meeting."

Lenihan's face crimsoned. His eyes averted Fargo's. "So what if I did?"

"I'd like to know what you talked about."

Lenihan pretended to adjust the string on the carpetbag. "I told them what people were saying. That maybe they were the robbers."

"What did they say to that?"

Lenihan met Fargo's gaze, held it for a moment. Then he sighed. "They lied to me."

"How'd you figure that out?"

"Like I said, I knew them since they were little kids. I asked them if they'd held up the stage and they said they hadn't but I knew better."

"And what did you do?"

"I told them that people thought I'd set it up for them. Told them about the money. I asked them to tell the truth. But then Clete—he was always the weakest one—he said if he told the truth they'd hang him. The driver and that Englishman died."

"What did the others do?"

"They told him to shut up. They told me he was lying. They told me to leave or they'd make trouble for me. They said if I told anybody what I knew they'd swear I was part of it and I'd hang, too."

"You should've gone to Cain."

From a stone ashtray on the counter Lenihan took a pipe. The bowl was comfortably blackened from years of smoking. He didn't light it. He just started turning it over and over in his hand. It was like a substitute for a rosary. Something to give him strength. "Think about it, Fargo. If I'd gone to Cain and he'd rounded up the boys they would have lied and told him I was part of it. He'd have made sure that I hung first. There was no way I could go to him."

"Not even when the boys started dying?"

"By then it was out of hand. The whole town thought I was in the middle of it. People who'd been my friends for years started acting suspicious around me, like I was a criminal they couldn't trust. The stage line even sent two men out here to interview me a week ago. There's a chance I'll be fired. I thought of asking Amy to leave town with me but if I left that would convince everybody I was guilty. And they'd follow me. No matter where I went, somebody from Cawthorne would keep track of me. And maybe someday they'd turn up some piece of fake evidence—" He stopped. He pointed to the bank bag with his pipe. "Like this."

"I've already shown this to Cain."

"So you think I'm guilty, too?"

"I think it looks bad for you. But I've got some doubts. I told Cain about them. You two hate each other so much there's no chance either one of you would listen to reason." Fargo dug into his pocket and pulled out the badge. "I even had him deputize me so I could bring you in myself."

"You're bringing me in?"

"That's my job."

"Once Cain gets his hands on me—"

"Pete Rule doesn't think you had anything to do with it."

"Pete's one of the few people who've stood by me."

"And I have my doubts. So I don't see how Cain can make any sudden moves. I was going to leave town myself but now I'm going to stay to see this through. You may be guilty but I haven't proved that to my own satisfaction yet. The bank bag looks sort of coincidental to me."

"Coincidental how?"

"The way it was buried. The fact that you kept it at all. You explained your meeting with the boys that night at the creek. I don't know if it's true but for now it sounds reasonable enough."

"What happens if Cain decides to shoot me when you or Pete aren't there? Tries to say I made a break for it or something?"

"Then I'll take care of Cain. And I'll tell him that when I bring you in."

"You talk like that to Tom Cain?"

Fargo shrugged. "We go back a ways. I know him pretty well. He's tough but not that tough and he wouldn't want to go up against me."

"He could be behind it, you know."

"You've said that and I've thought that. But right now I don't have any evidence of that. I want to talk to the Raines brothers. They're not very smart but you wouldn't have to be smart to set this up."

Lenihan shook his head. Stared down at the counter. "I thought everything was going to work out. Amy and I would get married and move in together. And then this robbery came up. It'll never be the same for us again, no matter how it turns out."

"Come on, close the place up. I'll take you down the alley so nobody'll see us."

"In handcuffs?"

"You think I'll need handcuffs?"

"I don't have a gun. Or a knife."

"Then I don't see any reason for them."

"I thought everything was going to work out," Lenihan said again.

Fargo watched as the stage line closed up for the night.

On the blackboard no coaches were scheduled to arrive until the next morning. Lenihan had a sheepskin coat. He shrugged into it after everything was set to order. Then he glumly blew out the lantern and they went outside and along the side of the building to the alley.

Fargo was glad that he didn't have to use handcuffs.

12

Pete Rule opened the back door of the sheriff's office.

The lantern in his hand poured light into the darkening alley, showing the worried face of Ned Lenihan. Fargo nudged the man inside with his Colt. Once inside, Rule bolted the door. He followed the other two up front to where Cain was talking to two of his night deputies.

Fargo had never seen them before. There was no doubt about what they were. Gunfighters. One middle-aged and worn, the other young and exuding cockiness and malice. They were both the type you used at night to keep the peace. You wouldn't want them on the prowl during daylight hours when the majority of decent citizens were out and about. Childish grins split their faces when they saw Lenihan. These two liked to gossip as much as anybody. Making sure everybody knew how important they were. And for sure within half an hour at least half the population of Cawthorne would know about Ned Lenihan being here.

"You boys get going now," Cain said, glancing at Lenihan and Fargo, trying to pretend that he wasn't especially interested in either of them. "It's dark and the fun'll start soon."

The two deputies kept grinning but they didn't say anything. They just walked to the door, took a final glance and went out.

Cain had been sitting on the edge of his desk. Now he went behind it and sat down. He indicated the bench on the right side of the door. This was where jail visitors sat waiting to go back to see their kin.

Fargo saw that Lenihan was shaking. And taking deep gulps of air. In the glow of the lanterns around the office his face glistened with sweat. The anger and resentment he'd expressed in the stage line office had disappeared once he'd confronted the reality of jail. Now there was just fear. This was real.

"Evening, Ned."

Lenihan gulped. "I didn't do anything, Cain, and you know it." But his voice shook as he spoke. Fargo was surprised Lenihan had been able to get out even these words.

"Remains to be seen, Ned. Remains to be seen." The pleasure he was taking with the smaller man irritated Fargo.

"You wanted him brought in. And here he is. You have some questions you want to ask him?"

"I was going to suggest you might need a lawyer, Ned," Cain said in that smirky drawl of his. "But if I didn't know better, I'd say you're already represented—by Fargo here."

"He says he had no idea that the bank bag was buried in his barn. He also admitted that as Rex Connor said he did see the three boys down at the creek right before they started dying. He told them he knew they'd robbed that stage and that they needed to confess. He did it because he wanted people to know that he didn't have anything to do with the robbery. The only way that could happen was if they told the truth. They threatened to tell you that he'd been part of it if he told anybody about them. He knew that you'd believe their story—or choose to believe it—if he went against them." He glanced down at Lenihan. "Is that about right, Lenihan?"

"I didn't do it, Cain. And you know it." Rallying a bit now, the anger coming back. "I don't know who planted that bag in my barn but I wouldn't be surprised if it was you."

"Well, counselor," Cain said ironically, "you got anything to say to that?"

"Nothing more than I've already said. That I'm not sure you're not behind all this."

"I'm afraid you're going to lose this case, counselor. Lenihan here is in financial straits; you've got a witness who saw him talking to those boys; and you found the bank bag on his property. And what kind of proof have you got that I had anything to do with it?"

"None—right now. But I'm going to keep looking around."

"And meantime I'll keep asking our friend here some questions of my own."

Lenihan's eyes showed his fear. "He could kill me and get away with it, Fargo. If you leave me alone with him—"

"I don't think you have anything to worry about, Lenihan." Fargo's slitted lake blue gaze bored into Cain's face. "Because Cain here knows that if anything happens to you while you're in his custody I'll come looking for him."

"That a threat?" Cain said.

"You damn right it is."

"A man could get downright jealous, you know that?" Cain said. "Here I thought Fargo and I were friends. But I guess he prefers you." He winked at Lenihan. "You be careful of him, though. He's got a way with the ladies. Amy might go for him."

"Shut up," Lenihan said. "I don't even like to hear you say her name."

Cain eased himself out of his chair. His face had hardened. And so had his voice. "I've had about enough of this, Fargo. You know damned well Lenihan here was part of the robbery and that he killed those three boys to keep them quiet. You've got all the evidence you need to impanel a jury and get a conviction. I don't know why you're so all hellfire hot to defend him like this but I'm telling you right now that it doesn't make any difference to me. I'm going to ask him some questions and then I'm going to lock him into a cell back there and then I'm going to send a runner to get Judge Mooney down here and tell him that I want to start proceedings right away. Now do we understand each other?"

Lenihan looked like a ten-year-old who'd just been deserted by his parents. He slumped forward and put his face in his hands.

"You take good care of him, Cain," Fargo said. "Or you'll be damned sorry."

Five steps out the front door of Cain's office a slender woman in a dark cotton dress and a yellow shawl, her head down and her body moving forward like a bullet, ran into Fargo and bounced off his chest. He grabbed her before she fell. In the spill light from the sheriff's window he saw the finely etched face of Amy Peters. Even with her years, even with the panic in her eyes, she was a beauty. In the darkening day, her shawl fell from her shoulders and she gaped up into the eyes of Fargo as if he were her direst enemy.

She ripped herself from his grasp. "You're the one! You're the one who arrested him! Those deputies came right to my house and told me!"

Stirring up trouble. And damned fast, too. Those two hadn't left more than ten, twelve minutes ago. They'd be traveling saloon to saloon now, making things as dramatic as possible. They were a perfect match for Cain.

"You need to calm down, lady."

"Calm down. Do you know what's going to happen to Ned in Tom Cain's jail?"

"Nothing's going to happen. I've warned Cain that if he doesn't keep Lenihan safe he'll answer to me."

Her angry laugh rang in the darkness. "And you're taking Tom Cain's word? If you had doubts why did you arrest him in the first place?"

"Because right now there are some things that point to him. Maybe he's innocent and maybe he's not. But there was enough evidence to bring him in."

"Of course he's innocent."

The door opened and Cain himself, silhouetted in the doorway, said, "Well, I have to say you're looking awfully pretty tonight, Amy."

She flew at the lawman before Fargo had time to react. She knocked him against the door frame and then clawed at him with her hands. In the light Fargo could see that she'd drawn two streaks of blood down one of Cain's cheeks.

Fargo started to grab her by the thin shoulders but before he could pull her back far enough Cain brought a fist up from nowhere and smashed her in the face. She fell backward into Fargo's arms and began sobbing. Fargo got her on her feet and then went after Cain, backhanding the man hard enough to evoke a real cry. Then he grabbed Cain by his fussy hair and slammed him back against the door frame twice. Then he hurled him into his office. Cain stumbled, sprawled across his desk. Lenihan was nowhere to be seen. Cain hadn't wasted any time putting Lenihan in a cell.

Fargo stomped into the office and jerked Cain to his feet. Then he threw him onto the bench where Fargo had sat with Lenihan. "You hit women now, do you, Tom? Probably felt real good, didn't it? The woman you wanted all these years and you finally got to show her what happens to women when they cross the great Tom Cain—or whatever the hell you're calling yourself these days. Now you're going to let her get Lenihan a good meal over to the café and let her sit in the cell with him while he eats it. And if I hear otherwise, you're going to be damned sorry because I'm going to this town council you talk about and tell them how you blackmailed a banker in one of the towns you cleaned up and left town with about a fourth of all the money in the bank. Maybe you've got a few things like that going here. In fact I'd bet on it."

As Lenihan had just a while ago, Cain looked shaken. But his trembling wasn't from fear but from rage. To be humiliated in front of the woman who had humiliated him—

Fargo drew Amy into the light. From what he could see, Cain's punch hadn't landed square. She touched her chin delicately but said, "I'm all right." Then to Cain, "If you hurt Ned in any way, you won't have to worry about Fargo. You'll have to worry about me. I'll kill you myself. And you know me well enough to know that's not an empty threat. Now I'm going to go get Ned a good meal and you'd damned well better do everything Fargo told you to."

She reached over and took Fargo's hand. "Now I know

that Ned's got at least one good friend besides me. Thank you."

Fargo scowled at Cain and walked out into the night.

The plate was filled with sliced potatoes, three thick slices of beef, beets. There was a deep cup of black coffee and there was a piece of apple cake in a paper napkin. A silver fork moved around on top of the feast, stopping first at the beef and then at the potatoes. Then the fork was set down on the coarse gray woolen blanket covering the cell cot and the hand reached for the cup of coffee.

Lenihan brought the coffee to his mouth, inhaled the steam. "This is good, Amy. Thanks."

Amy had never been in a jail cell before. She had had no idea how claustrophobic it was—and she would be able to leave. Then there were the smells. She didn't like to think about what had caused them. She could smell the sudsy cleaner somebody had mopped the floor with but that only added to the assault on her senses. And finally there was the laughter up front, on the other side of the heavy, closed door. She wondered if Cain had invited people in just so he could laugh with them and tease Ned and her. It would be like him. She had decided not to tell Ned that Cain had hit her. It would just make him angrier and more miserable.

Seeing that Ned hadn't touched his food, she said, "You need to eat, Ned."

"I wish I was hungry. But all I want is this cigarette and coffee." He'd forgotten his pipe but fortunately he'd brought along his makings.

"You don't know when you'll have your next meal."

Cain had let her bring a lantern into the cell. In the flickering light of it Ned appeared to be recovering from some injury or wound that had stunned him into deep shock. He spoke but the words were hollow. He saw her but he appeared to see something beyond her too. Some nightmare.

She took the plate from his lap and then picked up the knife and fork. She began to cut the beef as she once had for her little children. Tiny bites so they wouldn't choke. These were twice that size but still they might intimidate him less than large cuts of the meat.

She made a joke of it. When she'd cut several pieces she left the cot she'd been sitting on and seated herself next to him. "Now, my sweetheart, open wide."

"Oh, c'mon, Amy!"

"Open wide!"

The ridiculousness of the situation must have amused him because he actually smiled. And opened his mouth.

"Now chew."

"You are crazy."

"There's one bite. Open up again because here comes another one."

And so she fed him. He didn't eat all of it but he made a good dent in it. She thought it was endearing that he wolfed down the cake. He had a sweet tooth. Like a boy. All the time she was doing this, laughing and hearing him laugh, she was able to keep her sadness at bay. But when Ned was done with the meal and she had seated herself across from him again, the sorrow seized her. And she knew he recognized it in her eyes.

"I think Fargo's with me on this. I can see why he brought me in. I've been thinking about that. If I was a deputy I'd do the same thing. But I think he's got a lot of doubts, Amy, and I think that Cain's afraid of him. Fargo's not afraid to kill a man and I get the sense that he wouldn't mind killing Cain anytime the chance came up."

"I liked him, too, Ned. But I worry about Cain. Fargo can't be here to watch him all the time. I just hope that Cain decides it's not worth taking the chance to do anything to you."

"Well, Pete's around a lot of the time."

Mention of Pete Rule made her feel better. "That's right. I think he's on our side, too. That's what I've been told anyway. He stands up for you when people make accusations."

"That's what I mean."

But she could tell that he was more hopeful than actually convinced that Pete Rule could stop Cain.

The door opened. Laughter and smoke rolled into the shadows of the jail cells. Cain was outlined in the door with a glass of beer in his hand. His own laugh was as hearty as a pirate's.

Rubbing it in, she thought. Showing his contempt. She was glad she'd raked him across the cheek. She wished she'd done more damage. Except for protecting the lives of her children, Amy Peters had never had many violent thoughts. But she had them now. She felt she could cut Cain's throat and feel no remorse at all.

He ambled back, continuing his theatrical laugh. "I'm sorry you folks can't come up and join us. Well, I should say—that Ned can't come up and join us. Amy isn't a prisoner. She could come up but I doubt she'd want to. And it might not be safe. Four men with a lot of alcohol in them—"

He reached Lenihan's cell and put his face near the bars.

"What do you want?" Ned snapped.

"What I wanted and what I got seem to be two entirely different things, wouldn't you say, Ned? I tried to convince this lady that she'd be better off with me. And given how things have turned out, I'd say maybe I was right, wouldn't you, Amy?"

"Fargo's going to find out who's really behind all this," Amy said. "And I'm pretty sure he'll find out that it's you."

"Ah, yes, Fargo. I'd watch him, Ned. I can hear it in Amy's voice already. She's smitten with the man. That's how it usually goes with Fargo. You just can't trust him around women."

"I asked you what you want, Cain."

"Well, Ned, since you're so insistent—what I want is to tell you and Amy that visiting hours are over. I didn't have to let her back here to see you in the first place. Let alone let her bring you a fine meal. But now the time's up."

"I want you to let her out the back door."

"Now why would I do that, Ned?"

"Because I don't want her raped."

"You sure don't have much faith in me."

"I don't give a damn what you do to me, Cain. But let her out the back door."

"I hope you're touched by this, Amy. Your little friend here has gone noble on us. I don't know about you but I'm deeply moved by this. I didn't think the little man had it in him."

Amy swept up the plate and her purse and stalked to the door. "I don't know when or how, Cain, but I'm going to kill you with my own hands when this is all over."

"Then I take it this is the wrong time to ask you to marry me?"

Amy looked back at Ned. "I love you, Ned. I'll be back in the morning."

"Just to show you what a law-abiding lawman I am, Ned, I'm letting her out the back door. Even after she threatened to kill me. Now you be sure and tell Fargo what an upstanding lawman I am, will you?"

He laughed the whole time he lifted the heavy bolt off the door and let her out into the alley.

13

Pushing through the batwings Fargo saw how crowded the Gold Mine saloon was. The long bar was packed as were the tables. On the surface this might have been nothing more than one of those nights when a large number of men decided to spend a little time drinking before going home to their families and supper. But that would have meant a jovial mood among most of the drinkers and the mood here was anything but jovial. The sure sign of this was how none of the drinkers paid any attention to any of the saloon girls. Usually they'd be joshing with them or flirting with them. A few of them would be going upstairs to partake of their services.

But not tonight. Tonight there would be only one topic of conversation. And that would be Ned Lenihan.

When the bartender saw Fargo, he shouted, "Here's the man who brought him in!"

A few dozen shouts went up in the smoky air. A couple of men near Fargo patted him on the back. Admiration and appreciation shone in every eye. Fargo was the man of the hour.

By the time he reached the bar, the bartender had his schooner ready for him. Two men parted to make room for him. The bartender said, "This town owes you a debt of gratitude, Mr. Fargo."

"Well, time will tell."

"Well, you got him, didn't you?"

"We'll have to see."

The conversations around him stopped. Men wanted to

hear what Fargo was saying. And Fargo wanted to be heard. Though law and order had come to a good part of the frontier, the people of Cawthorne had lived through a frightening month. Three of their own young men dead. And the lingering and ever-increasing suspicion that Ned Lenihan, one of the most trusted people in the entire town, was behind it all. The rage would be setting in just about now. Fargo had seen it too many times. One or two of the men would start stirring up the others, suggesting that they had the right to take the law into their own hands. Suggesting that maybe even Tom Cain himself would throw in with them. Suggesting that since Ned Lenihan had killed some of their own—that they had the right to kill Lenihan themselves, to hell with judges and juries. At first most of the men would disagree. They would rightly see these men as hotheads, as troublemakers. But one by one and then two by two and then in larger numbers the other men would give in to their own anger, the alcohol consumed only making it easier to do so, and what had been unthinkable a few hours ago would now seem like the absolute right thing to do.

"You don't sound real sure about Lenihan, Fargo," the bartender said.

"I'm not. He might be guilty and he might not."

"Well, you arrested him, didn't you?" The man was chunky but powerful-looking with angry dark eyes and a black beard. "That's good enough for me. Far as I'm concerned he's the one who killed my cousin Clete."

"This is Dave Teale, Fargo. He's only a shirttail kin of Clete but he makes it sound like they was brothers."

The men around him laughed.

"You think it's funny, do you?" There was real peril in his voice—peril for the bartender. And the bartender knew it. He moved back a few steps. Dave Teale had the floor. "You arrest a man and you're not sure he's guilty? Meaning what—that you could let him go?"

"That's how it works sometimes. You arrest a man but then later you find out he wasn't guilty so you let him go."

"Well, I say he's guilty." He shouted at all the men in the

saloon, men now paying close attention because they thought there might be a fight about to happen. And who wanted to turn down a good old fight?

In every town, burg, city there were Dave Teales. Hell, even in Washington, D.C., there were Dave Teales. Men who weren't satisfied unless they were rattling sabers and stirring up trouble. Here was a man who was Clete Byrnes' shirttail kin—if that—and he was talking like the boy had been his blood brother. And the men listening to him, genuinely angry over the events of the past weeks but also bored and looking for relief from their everyday lives, heard in Teale the voice of the righteous and reasonable. A man was arrested therefore the man was guilty. Later, after more alcohol had been consumed, Teale would push for his real purpose— to demand that Cain let Teale and his men take care of Lenihan themselves. In every town, burg, city there were Dave Teales.

Since Teale had been addressing the men, Fargo took a turn at it. "Maybe Teale here's right. Maybe Lenihan is guilty. But he's behind bars and you can bet that Cain won't let him go. So there's nothing to worry about. If you think Lenihan is guilty then you can rest easy because there won't be any more killings. You and your families can rest easy."

The men were still sober enough that Fargo won them to his side—temporarily at least. He could see in their faces that his words had made sense to them. For now, anyway, they realized that the situation was well in hand. But a long night was ahead and Fargo wondered how long they'd stay reasonable.

Teale shook his head. "It ain't right. Why should he draw even one more breath when them three boys are dead?"

"Well, if you're right, Teale, I imagine Lenihan won't be drawing a breath as soon as his trial's over."

"Trial? You sound like you're on his side, Fargo."

"Teale, you're starting to piss me off."

Teale snorted his disdain for the Trailsman but he didn't say anything.

Fargo looked directly at Teale. "I'll be headed back this

way real soon and I don't want to see you trying to start any trouble. You hear me?"

To emphasize his point he thumped Teale on the chest with his knuckles. Then he nodded to the bartender and left.

The words came in torrents, in gushes. And they were good words, fine words, the best words since O'Malley had been working in Chicago before he turned into a human whiskey bottle. He sat at his wobbly desk in his cell-like hotel room, a lantern at hand, his pen scratching out a steady rhythm. He had within reach not a whiskey bottle but a cup of steaming coffee. His moment had come at last and he wanted nothing to spoil it.

The story began with the revelation of the killer's name. After that was a recap of everything that had taken place over the past weeks. He noted how Lenihan was set up by whispers as the guilty man. The story read like a piece concocted by Edgar Allan Poe.

There in the golden glow of the lantern a rebirth was taking place. Maybe he'd be drinking again very soon. Maybe the old ways were just too difficult to change. What would the world look like through sober eyes? he wondered. He smiled to himself. Maybe it would be like staring directly into the sun—blinding him. He'd always told himself that in the bottle was truth. Maybe he'd been wrong—maybe in the bottle were lies, self lies.

He laughed out loud. Hell, here he was carrying on when he didn't know if he could go as long as eight hours without a drink and he was planning a dry future for himself.

He sat back in his chair and looked at the pages in front of him. He felt pride. The same kind of pride he'd had as a young man getting scoops in Chicago.

He was so absorbed in reading his words that he didn't hear the door open behind him. Wasn't aware of another presence in the room until the killer had taken two steps across the threshold.

Then, shocked, O'Malley turned and met the eyes of the

person he'd been writing about. They seemed to gleam in the shadows beyond the glow of the lantern.

"You dropped something when you paid me a visit."

O'Malley was unarmed. No reason to carry a gun when he was in his own room. Unarmed—and there could be only one reason the killer had come here.

The killer came up to the edge of the light. He held a business card in his hand. The card identified the paper and the owner Parrish. Parrish didn't think enough of O'Malley to have his name printed on them.

"I doubt it was Parrish who was there. So that leaves you."

O'Malley's eyes began searching the darkness for some way to avoid the inevitable. The killer had not yet shown a gun but it was certain he had one. Inevitable. What could O'Malley do? All he could think of was diving at the killer's legs, surprising him, knocking him over and then running to the door and the hall and shouting for help. There were people around at this hour. People with guns. People who might not care for him but who would protect him on general principle.

But the body had been abused for so long, what if he tried to make a dive and did nothing more than land at the killer's feet? His situation would be hopeless then. But then, he thought, what was it now?

"How did you figure it out?"

"I saw you one day and got curious. How you handled something." What was the point of pretending anymore?

"How I handled what?"

So O'Malley told him. How the killer's behavior had made him curious about the break-in at the woman's house. How the man had watched the woman.

And then how O'Malley had begun studying the man every chance he got. In the old days when he'd worked on the big-city papers he'd begun making a study of people arrested for crimes. A lot of them would never be suspected. Nice normal ordinary people. Or so they seemed. But at their trials O'Malley began to see what they'd kept hidden about themselves. And how clever their masks were.

"I'm impressed, O'Malley. I figured you were just one more drunken reporter. It seems your kind always like the bottle too much. But you must be a lot smarter than I realized. How long have you suspected me?"

"Ever since the break-in. But I wasn't sure and I couldn't prove it. I didn't have any real evidence until I found that box under your couch. It's kind of funny, keeping all those things of hers. Sort of sad, too."

"Shut up. I don't want you talking about her. Somebody like you shouldn't even mention her name."

He's crazy, O'Malley thought. He's crazy as a loon.

"I want the box, O'Malley."

"I imagine you do. But I can't give it to you. I've already given it to Fargo."

"Fargo? You're lying."

O'Malley supposed it was a pretty pathetic lie. The box was sitting on the nightstand by his bed. The darkness hid it.

The killer brushed past him then. The room was so small that he was able to reach the bed and the nightstand in seconds. His harsh laugh told O'Malley that he'd found the box.

"So Fargo has it, huh?"

O'Malley was turning around in his chair as the killer cinched on his black leather gloves and stepped forward. O'Malley didn't even have a chance of defending himself. The killer's hands were so powerful that they snapped the trachea instantly. There was no problem then in finishing the job.

After he was sure O'Malley was dead, Deputy Pete Rule tucked the box under his arm and hurried from O'Malley's hotel room.

14

As soon as Helen Hardesty heard a horse approaching her cabin, she ran for the rifle she had left leaning against the large oak that stood near the garden she had been tending. At age sixty-four, Helen had survived two husbands and the death of three of her nine children. She lived alone now by choice because in her later years she no longer wanted the complications of human relationships. Even when you loved someone, he or she could be burdensome. Her intimates now were her pinto, her wolfhound and her four cats. She had birdsong for music and magnificent mountain sunsets for beauty.

And until recently she'd had safety and comfort.

If only she hadn't been tramping through the thin stand of jack pines. . . . She hadn't meant to see him or what he was doing. In fact she tried to run and hurry away from what he was about to do to the terrified young man she recognized as Clete Byrnes. She had seen him around town when she went in for supplies. He was now tied to a slender oak. She also knew the man holding the gun on him. She knew she could not get involved. He would kill her for sure. She would have to pretend that she didn't know anything about it. And so be it. She probably didn't have that many years left and she wanted to live them out peacefully. With her mountain sunsets and her animals.

But as she started away her foot found a hole and threw her into the bushes. The noise alerted the man with the gun. He came for her. He slapped her over and over again until her knees buckled and he had to drag her to her cabin.

"I'm going to take care of some business here, Helen. It's business that don't concern you. And it's business you'd damned well better keep to yourself or I'll kill you. You understand me, Helen? I'll kill you and I'll get away with it, too. And you know I will."

The funny thing was he didn't even sound angry when he said all this. He was just stating a fact.

"Now you just sit here and I'll do it quick and get it over with. And you stay away from that spot by those trees down by the creek. No need for you to see what I done. You understand, Helen?"

"Yes."

"Somebody'll come by soon enough and find him. And they'll come and ask you if you know anything about it and you know what to say. You understand, Helen?"

"Yes."

"You tell them you don't know anything about it."

"No."

"Because if you did tell them anything, I'd have to kill you. And I think you know me well enough that I wouldn't want to do that. You know me that well, don't you, Helen?"

"Yes, I do, Pete."

And then sitting there when he went away. And five minutes later the explosion of three gunshots. And then a terrible mountain silence.

And now, three days later, nervous every time she heard a horse on the trail that angled by her land.

By the time she could see the rider, she had her rifle up and aimed and ready to fire.

Fargo his name was. The man on the big Ovaro stallion. The man with those striking lake blue eyes. A good man, she'd sensed the other day, but a man who asked too many questions. A man who could get her in trouble. He was golden in the moonlight, a creature of myth as in some of the books she'd read as a little girl.

She shouted, "You better stop right there!"

* * *

This was pretty much the same situation Fargo had faced when he'd first laid eyes on Helen Hardesty. The harsh shout. The belligerent face. The rifle.

She whistled. From the shadows next to the house the wolfhound came running, lean and purposeful. He stood next to her. "He'll kill you if I tell him to."

"I don't have much time, Helen." He walked toward her.

"You stop right there."

"There could be a lynching in town tonight. An innocent man could die unless you tell me who you saw murder the Byrnes boy."

"Who said I saw anything?"

"The way you're acting, Helen. You're hiding something. Something you're scared about. My guess is that the killer has threatened you. And you don't scare easy. So that means he must have some kind of power. He thinks—and you think—that he can kill you and get away with it."

The night winds soughed in the trees and filled the air with the scent of pine and the snow that had fallen on the lower parts of the mountains. A good night for sleeping in a warm bed. Sounded pretty good to Fargo.

"Who's the man they're going to lynch?"

"Ned Lenihan."

"Ned Lenihan!" she said. "Why, he's one of the most decent people I've ever known. He's a good man. He was friends with both of my husbands."

"Well, there's some evidence against him so I had to bring him in. Now I'm wondering if I should have."

He moved closer to her. A deep growl sounded in the wolfhound's throat but it remained still.

"Three men are dead, Helen. Their families deserve some answers."

"Well, I'm sorry for the families, Fargo. But I don't have no answers to give."

An owl flew downwind, elegant against the moonlight sky.

"Maybe you're trusting the wrong people, Helen."

"What's that supposed to mean?"

"Maybe you're scared to tell the truth because somebody threatened you."

"You're wrong there, Fargo. I'm not scared of nobody. I didn't know that body was anywhere near here."

"Look, Helen, you've lived out West a long time—maybe all your life. You know how animals respond to something like a human body. You've got a dog and cats and you probably get around your land pretty much every day. Kind of hard to believe that Clete Byrnes could have laid out there without you knowing anything about it. Unless you stayed inside your house for a couple days."

The rifle lowered a few inches. "I don't have many years left. I want to die peaceful. Enjoying myself. I don't think that's asking a lot." Outlined in the silver light of the half-moon she looked small and bent. Her usual vigor was gone.

"I don't think you want to die knowing that Ned Lenihan was sentenced for three killings he didn't commit. That wouldn't make for a very peaceful life. You're too good a woman to live with something like that hanging over you."

"How about the threat of death hanging over me?"

"I can take care of whoever's threatening you, Helen. Take care of him once and for all."

The sigh indicated that she was shifting toward telling him. He had kept his voice gentle, reasonable. "Whoever he is, Helen, he's going to kill you one way or another. He has to. You're the one person he fears. The one person who can tell the truth about him. Maybe he won't kill you right away but he *will* kill you. That you can bet on."

She was silent a moment. He could see her eyes watching him, wondering about him. She'd want to know if he really would protect her, if he really could protect her. He didn't blame her. A woman her age and all alone, she was especially vulnerable.

He would never know if she had made up her mind to confide in him or not. The rifle shots cracked in the darkness. Before he could push her to the ground and out of the path of the bullets, he saw her forehead split open like a chasm. She wobbled backward on her feet and then fell forward into Fargo's arms. He grabbed her and held her as he flung them both to the ground, rolling, constantly rolling, as the continued shots tried to pick them off. The gunman was in a stand of jack pines.

"Dammit, Sam. You missed Fargo."

Kenny and Sam Raines. The slimiest bastards in Cawthorne.

There was nothing he could do for Helen now so he eased his arms from her, sensing that her life force had already left her body. He wanted to be more reverent with her but there was no time. There were two men he was going to kill.

Amy Peters forced her way to the front of the crowd that had gathered outside the sheriff's office. To her the sight was as lurid as the illustrations in cheap magazines. Around thirty drunken men, some of them holding torches, shouting for Tom Cain to let them have Ned Lenihan for a hanging. The stink of kerosene was on the air as the torch flames whipped in the wind. The faces of the men were cold and grotesque from their anger. Several of them held pint bottles of rotgut whiskey in their hands. A few waved pistols. Cain had drawn the curtains and had made no appearance. To Amy this meant he was expecting the worst and was hunkering down. She was afraid that he'd give in to them. He'd pretend that he didn't have any choice but would secretly be happy to see them drag Ned out of his cell and push him down the street to where the old hanging tree sat behind the general store.

She shouted, "Listen to me! Listen to me!"

Her words made them only more belligerent. They shouted back, "Get out of here, Amy, unless you want to get hurt!" "You know he's a killer but you just won't admit it!" "He deserves to die and you're not gonna stop us!"

One drunkard even rushed for her but a larger man grabbed him by the collar of his denim jacket and pulled him back.

Amy stood in a flat-brimmed black hat, a sheepskin, a red sweater and jeans. To show that she was serious, a Colt dangled from the fingers of her left hand. Only now were a few of them beginning to notice her gun. She decided to let the others know in a dramatic way. She angled the gun so that the bullet would pass safely over their heads. And then she fired.

They stopped shouting. Drunken ears rang with the sound of the gunshot. Drunken eyes narrowed, fixed on the pretty woman standing in front of the sheriff's door.

"I want you to listen to this. Sheriff Cain himself asked Skye Fargo to look into the killings. Fargo found enough evidence to arrest Ned. But Fargo is the first to admit that most of the evidence seems shady. As if somebody had set Ned up. And if you don't believe me you can ask Fargo."

"Fargo don't live here!" a man bellered, his Stetson painted a reddish-gold from the torch he held. "And he ain't got no right to decide what happens in this town!"

The rumble went through the crowd again, animals making threatening noises to their perceived enemy, the woman who was defending the man they wanted to lynch.

"You men need to wait until you're sober! You don't want to do anything you'll regret!"

"Who said we'll regret it?" a man shouted.

And the crowd laughed.

Amy wanted to empty her gun into them. Stupid, drunken animals, all of them.

The door opened behind her. She turned to see Tom Cain, a sawed-off shotgun in one hand, step out onto the plank walk and stand next to her.

"We want you to let us have him, Cain!"

"And right now! Right damn now!"

"He's the killer and you know it!"

Cain said, "Amy's right. We don't want any lynching here. This is a law-and-order town. And I mean to keep it that way."

Amy was surprised by how confident and certain he sounded. There was a real threat in his voice. But then he turned to her and even before he spoke his face parted into a grin, his sneering grin, and he said, "Of course I can't hold these boys off forever. They get ten more out here I'll have to turn him over. I'm not going to sacrifice my men for the sake of Lenihan."

He'd said it loudly enough for everybody to hear.

A boisterous cheer went up. They'd have their hanging soon enough.

15

The Raines boys were having trouble finding Fargo now. He'd rolled out of the direct line of fire, forcing Sam to shift positions in order to find him in the darkness. Sam kept reloading and firing. Fargo didn't return fire. They were out of range of his Colt. He swung wide. His intent was to surprise them. They were so intent on killing him that they'd kept searching the shadows for him, staying in the same location the whole time.

Their horses were ground-tied on the downslope of the hill the Raines boys were using. He decided to use the horses as a way of luring the two out of their sanctuary.

He crept up to the animals, his Colt at the ready, tied the reins and looped them over the saddle horns. "Git," he ordered, swatting both horses on their rumps. The horses whinnied and trotted off.

In the vast mountain silence, in the moonlight-limned gloom of the trees where the duo was hiding, a shout went up, "What the hell spooked our horses?"

By this time Fargo had edged up the hill and tucked himself inside the line of jack pines. They wouldn't know where he was until it was too late. He got within range of them and let them start down the hill. When their backs were to him, he said, "Drop your rifle right now, Sam, or I'll shoot you where you stand."

He had to give them some time to realize that they'd walked into a trap. They froze in place. Fargo imagined they were considering their chances. There were two of them.

They could pitch their bodies in different directions and Fargo might have a hard time finding them with his gun. And maybe they'd get lucky. Maybe one or both of them could kill Fargo before he killed either one of them.

"What're you gonna do to us?" Sam Raines said.

"Put your rifle down real slow, Sam. Set it on the ground. And then both of you empty your holsters the same way."

Obviously Kenny hadn't been able to manipulate a rifle with his left hand but that wouldn't stop him from using a six-shooter.

"I didn't mean to shoot that old woman. I was aiming for you, Fargo."

"Shut up, Sam. You make me sick when you whine."

"Well, it's true."

"Put the rifle down now. And the guns right after. Real slow."

"You gonna kill us?" Sam Raines said.

"I'd like to but if you give yourselves up I'll just take you in."

"Now!" Kenny Raines shouted.

He was quicker and more agile than Fargo would have given him credit for. Kenny Raines dove to his left, dragging his six-shooter out at the same time. Before he even reached the ground he'd squeezed off two shots, both of them burning close to Fargo's head. The blazing red-yellow flame of the explosions seemed to linger on the shadows.

Fargo took to the ground himself. He slammed his head down as two more bullets blazed past his flattened body. Kenny Raines was a resourceful gunfighter. No doubt about that.

But then he made his mistake. Fargo read it instinctively. Down to two bullets, Kenny Raines had to take a real chance now. He had to raise himself up very quickly to get a better angle at Fargo. He had to bet he could get his shots off before Fargo got his.

He lost the bet. Fargo pumped three bullets into the man's chest. Kenny screamed as the bullets tore into him. His entire body danced before he settled onto the ground. Fargo was pretty sure he'd heard the word "Mama!" cried as the gunfighter was dying.

Sam Raines stood near his brother with his arms raised above his head. "I don't want to die, Fargo. I'm sorry I killed that old woman."

"Walk over here and keep your hands up. I'm going to tie you up and send somebody back here for you. And the way I'll tie you up there won't be any way you can escape. Believe me. Now move."

Sam Raines began walking toward Fargo. He'd gone four steps exactly when Fargo saw what was taking place behind Sam. "You coward!" Kenny Raines called out. He had only the strength to raise the gun he'd somehow managed to hold on to and then pull the trigger twice, exploding his brother's head into chunks. He tried to take aim at Fargo but the Trailsman was way ahead of him. He did the same thing to Kenny that Kenny had done to Sam. This time the exploding pieces of bone and brain weren't quite as spectacular.

But you couldn't have everything.

16

Fargo could hear the mob before he saw it.

Human roars ebbed and flowed as he approached the hill that overlooked Cawthorne. Shouts and screams, even a few gunshots punctuated what should have been bedtime silence. Disturbing as the sounds were, they signified that Lenihan probably hadn't been dragged out of his prison cell as yet. They were likely still trying to get inside the sheriff's office.

As soon as he reached the top of the hill, he saw that he was right. The area around the sheriff's office was crowded with bodies, torches, rifles. He could almost smell the alcohol from here. A dangerous situation that liquor would keep making more dangerous.

The plank walk in front of Cain's office was empty. Cain and Rule and the two night deputies would be inside, their shotguns ready. One question was how long they could hold out. The other question was did Cain really *want* to hold out? Even if he knew that Amy would never go with him, he probably wouldn't mind seeing Lenihan hang. After all, Ned had done the unthinkable—at least in Cain's mind—Lenihan had humiliated him.

Fargo knew better than to ride down the main street with Helen Hardesty's blanket-wrapped body over the back of his horse. That would only incite more rage. She had died without telling him who she'd seen kill Clete Byrnes. He doubted it was the Raines brothers. They'd come to Helen's to kill him, not Helen. And given what he'd learned about them it was unlikely that the three robbers would ever have gotten involved with them. The boys had been wild but not stupid.

And the Raines boys, for all their bravado, had not been blessed with brains.

He swung wide so that he would come in behind the main street. There were a few large barns that functioned as warehouses and a handful of shacklike homes strewn out across the dusty flatland. He could reach the back door of the sheriff's office without being seen. If there were some mob members back there he'd have to deal with them any way he could.

The shouts and screams were hellish as he made his way past the warehouses and approached the sheriff's office. The flames from the torches burnished the night sky with a lurid gold-red color.

He was happy to see that nobody lurked behind Cain's office. The entertainment—and that was part of any lynching—was out front. If Cain was any kind of a lawman, and he was, he'd have somebody stationed at the back door with a sawed-off. There'd be hell to pay for anybody who tried to break in.

Fargo dropped from the saddle, ground-tied his Ovaro and hurried to the back door. He pounded on the door and shouted, "It's Fargo! Let me in!" He didn't have to worry about yelling too loud. The crowd voices easily covered his own.

It took three tries before he heard the heavy wooden bar being lifted from the door. A deputy with a white ten-gallon hat and a cigar butt jammed into the corner of his mouth kept his sawed-off trained on Fargo. The deputy stepped to the threshold, gaped around and then stood back to let Fargo inside.

"They'll be making their move any time now," the deputy said. "My name's Hal Parsons by the way. I've heard a lot about you." He nodded to the front of the place. "They're all up front. I'm stationed here."

"Don't trust Parsons, Fargo," Ned Lenihan said, his hands gripping the bars of his cell. "He's one of Cain's gunnies. I heard them talking earlier. They're going to turn me over to the mob, Fargo. You've got to help me."

"You're lucky I don't come in there and kill you myself, Lenihan," Parsons snapped. He was tall, a powerful man starting to show middle age.

"You sure you're a deputy?" Fargo said.

Parsons smirked. "Friend of his, are you, Fargo?"

"As a matter of fact I am."

Amy Peters was slumped on the bench in front of Cain's desk. Cain and Rule stood on either side of the door, rifles in their hands. Not until he was closer to Amy did he notice the fresh bruise on her cheek.

"What happened to Amy?" Fargo said as soon as he saw the injury.

Cain and Rule glanced at each other.

"I got angry out there trying to calm them down," Cain said. "I backhanded her because she was just adding to the pressure."

Fargo walked over to Amy. She sat up. He reached under her chin and tilted her face toward him so he could see the bruise better.

He stood less than three inches from Cain and said, "Why don't you try and backhand me and see what happens?"

"It was a mistake, all right? This is a dangerous situation."

The only warning that Fargo got was Amy's scream. That was the last sound he heard after Parsons' six-shooter slammed across the back of his skull and drove him to the floor.

"Here's some water."

Fargo opened his eyes to see Ned Lenihan standing over him with a tin cup in his hand. The stench told Fargo where he was. A cell.

"They must have knocked you out. They brought you back here. Parsons and Cain. I guess they figured you'd get in the way when they let the crowd come in and get me."

"Thanks." Fargo accepted the cup. He sat up on the edge of the cot and drank it down. Inside his skull a knife sawed through his brain.

The mob had broken into a chant. "Hand him over now!"

Lenihan had a pale, shaken look to him. He moved with great effort. He returned to his own cot and sat down and put his face in his hands. "It's going to happen. They're going to hang me. And I didn't do it, Fargo. I really didn't."

"I believe you, Lenihan."

"Cain's waited all this time to pay me back for Amy. He acted like I'd stolen her from him. He's crazy when it comes to this. Insane, I mean."

The door separating the front office from the jail cells opened. Pete Rule said, "I'll make sure they're not up to anything."

"What the hell are they going to be up to?" Cain said. "Neither of them has a gun."

"You're forgetting who Fargo is."

Rule strode to the cell. He faced the two men and put a finger to his lips, signaling silence. Then he reached inside his shirt and pulled out a Colt. He waved for Fargo to come to the cell door. He whispered, "A lot of this is my fault. I should've told you the truth. Cain's behind all this. He set up the robbery with the boys. He took all the money. I heard him talking to one of them right after the stickup."

Fargo didn't know who he wanted to kill first. Cain for the robbery and the killings or Rule for letting it get this far.

But it was Rule who slipped the six-shooter through the bars and let Fargo take it. Better late than never. At least he was making up for it now.

More whispering. "I'm going up front. I'll leave the door open slightly. You can get the drop on them."

"What the hell are you doing back there?" Cain shouted. "I need you up here."

True enough, the roar of the mob was now almost deafening. Men were hurling things at the front of the office. Fargo heard glass shatter. He reasoned that they were minutes away from Cain throwing open the door and letting them take Lenihan. He'd make a show of it. He'd give a good law-and-order speech that nobody would hear for the din. But at least he could boast after the hanging that he'd made his plea.

Rule unlocked the cell door quietly then hurried up front. As promised, he left the door open slightly.

Gun in hand, Fargo said, "You stay here. I'll take care of Cain and Parsons and then come back."

"I could help."

"No. Stay here. I'll move faster alone."

Fargo slipped out of the cell and started moving carefully toward the door. He had no specific plan. He had to see where everybody was positioned before he could make a move.

The angle the door afforded him wasn't helpful at first. He heard them talking under the din of the mob but he couldn't see anybody, not even Rule.

He had to battle his own impatience. All this grief caused by Cain.

Hurry up, you son of a bitch. Move across the floor so I can see you.

A long minute and a half dragged by before Fargo saw the back of Parsons' head. Now he could move. He jerked the door open and said, "If you move, Parsons, I'll shoot you in the back."

Then he lunged into the office, checking on Cain as he did so. Cain was sitting in his chair. He was in no position to draw and fire before Fargo could kill him.

"Get their guns, Pete," Fargo said.

"Pete!" Cain said. Shock strained his voice and gaze. "Pete—you threw in with Fargo?"

"Yeah. And I told him who was behind the robbery, too. You're behind this whole thing."

"What the hell're you talking about?"

But Fargo could see and hear the truth. For all his acting skills, Cain's face revealed that Rule's words were factual.

As Rule collected Parsons' gun and bowie knife, Fargo faced Cain. "Take the Colt out and slide it across the desk."

"I just wanted some money before I left town, Fargo. My time's passed. It was just going to be a simple robbery. I didn't plan for the driver or that Englishman to get killed.

One of the boys got scared and shot them accidentally. That's what they told me and I believed them. I—"

He was pushing his Colt across the desk as he spoke. The gun was just about at the far edge of the desk when the door crashed. Wood shattered. The walls shook. A torch was hurled into the office through the battered center of the door. Two railroad ties bound together with leather straps collided with the door again, splintering it completely in two. Axes hacked away the rest and three crazed men stumbled through the door frame.

One of them surged forward. Fargo grabbed him. Turned him around. Jammed the barrel of his Colt against the man's head.

"One more step and I kill him."

"You can't kill us all."

"No, but I can kill him." He had his arm around the man's neck. He tightened his grip. "Tell your friends you don't want to die."

The two men raised their own guns but paused when they heard their friend's gibbering. Fargo's captive said, "He'll do it. Just stay where you are!"

The problem for the two men—and for the captive—was the men behind them, trying to push their way through the shattered door into the sheriff's office.

Fargo said, "Ned Lenihan is innocent. The man you want is sitting right at that desk. Sheriff Cain confessed just a minute ago."

"Fargo! It's not what you're thinking!" Cain started to say.

From Fargo's vantage point he couldn't tell what Cain was doing. Pete Rule was covering the man.

And it was Pete Rule's gun that cracked two times in the tumult of the screaming mob, the standoff between Fargo and the two men facing him and Amy's sudden cry.

"I thought he was going for a gun."

Fargo angled his head so that he could see Tom Cain fall facedown on his desk. One of his eyes had been shot out, his cheek running with blood. His forehead leaked blood too.

His face colliding with the desktop would have made a grim sound under ordinary circumstances. But all the clamor covered it.

Fargo released the man he was holding and threw him into his friends. "You people make me sick. Now get the hell out of here." As he said this, he dug the deputy's badge out of his pocket and pitched it on Rule's desk. "It's all yours, Pete. It's up to you. I'm going to go get a lot of whiskey and get out of this town by dawn."

"I'm sorry for all this, Fargo."

Fargo glanced over at Lenihan who was holding Amy so tight they looked like one person. He didn't blame him. Lenihan was lucky to be alive. "I'm taking Helen Hardesty's body over to the mortuary. The Raines boys tried to kill me but they killed her instead. You'll find their bodies out on her property. I'll pay for Helen's burial. The town doesn't have to worry about it."

"You don't have to do that, Fargo."

"Yeah," Fargo said, "I do."

"Mr. Fargo—" Amy said from the arms of Lenihan. "We owe you so much—"

Fargo turned then and walked over to Deputy Parsons. Before the man could protect himself Fargo slammed his right hand into his solar plexus and finished with a left hand to his jaw. Parsons crashed backward into a chair, filling the air with his curses.

Fargo was sick of it all. He just wanted to get the hell out of there.

17

The bourbon was good, the fireplace warmed the elegant living room and Sarah Friese was quietly erotic as she sat next to Fargo on the long brocaded couch. The first and second floors of the mortuary might be dedicated to death but the third floor was very much given over to life. One wall was filled with a built-in bookcase, the other walls were covered with expensive reproductions of paintings by the masters and a genuine Persian rug covered most of the shiny hardwood floor. West of this room was a dining area as fancy as that of a top-flight San Francisco hotel. This was where she'd served him the steak dinner she'd insisted on preparing for him in the shiny new kitchen.

For Fargo two hours up here had softened his harsh feelings toward the town itself. He'd left the sheriff's office bitter and angry. He'd stayed pretty much the same way while Sarah worked on Helen Hardesty's body and prepared her for burial. But the whiskey and the fire helped as he waited for Sarah to bathe and reappear in a deep blue robe that fit her so well that he could easily see she was naked beneath. Now, as she'd said, she was all Fargo's.

He turned to her and smiled. "This is quite the place."

"My flat. My father and mother live in a house nearby. I wanted my own life. I'm not quite as old-fashioned as they are. And anyway, I wanted you to have a decent meal before you left town. We owe you a lot. Lynching is bad enough but lynching the wrong man is something a lot of towns never get over."

"Well, Pete Rule finally told the truth. He should have done it a lot earlier."

"At least he did it."

"I'm just sorry Helen Hardesty had to die. She died because of me. Those damned Raines brothers are the ones who should've been lynched."

She touched his face with silken fingers, the subtle scent of her perfume a perfect match for her graceful beauty. "You're getting yourself all worked up again, Skye. You need to relax."

He smiled. "You have any idea of how you could relax me?"

"Well, I'm only nineteen but I think if I put my mind to it I could come up with something."

"You have anything particular in mind?"

She eased herself close to him, let her fingers fall from his face to tease his burgeoning manhood in the crotch of his pants. He gave a little start, pleasure spreading through his body like fine wine. Then her mouth was on his and she was finding his tongue with her own. By now he had filled his right hand with one of her breasts and he was easing her back on the long couch so that their bodies could fit together. Her robe rode up on her long, firm thighs so Fargo had no problem stirring the hot, moist center of her. She began to strain against him, wanting him inside her, her mouth filling his with warm wine-soaked gasps of pleasure and anticipation.

He obliged her first, his expert tongue tasting the elixir of her youthful beauty, her responding with cries, sobs and even a scream when her mind burst into a fireworks display of fleshly joy.

She helped him shed his pants so that she could hold his massive ramrod and guide it into her. "Oh, God, Skye, you're huge." She laughed about it. "I'll have to mark this date on my calendar."

But then she was serious again, spreading herself beneath him so that he could blaze a path up inside her that would fulfill the crazed need they both felt.

She got her slender, perfect legs over his shoulders and grabbed his buttocks. He grabbed hers. They were wet with her own juices. And then they embarked on their long journey, taking and giving by turns, the scents and sensations of their passion the only reality for either of them.

The expensive couch was never going to be the same as they pounded and slammed their way to mutual ecstasy, his mouth on her nipple only making her luxuriate all the more in the endless orgasms she was enjoying.

Then, as all things must, their coupling came to an end. Because the couch was so confining, Fargo let himself slide to the floor. He lay back against the couch and rooted around in his clothes for his makings.

Just as he was lighting his smoke, she joined him. She pleased him with her clean, young laugh. "You may have spoiled me for life."

"I doubt that."

She took his cigarette from his hand and put it to her own lips. She inhaled deeply then erupted in a coughing fit.

He took the cigarette from her when she was still hacking. "Little girls shouldn't smoke."

"I'll get the hang of those things one of these days." Then: "There's more wine."

"I'd better pass. I need to get up real early. I'm going to be out of here by dawn."

"It's not that late."

"It's that late if I want to get a full day's travel in. I've got friends waiting for me. And besides, I've got one more stop to make tonight."

Her blue eyes sparkled with mischief. "It'd better not be another woman."

"Oh, no. It's O'Malley."

"O'Malley," she said. "He's sort of a joke around here. But I've always felt sorry for him."

"Same here. He was so fired up about this whole thing but I didn't see him anywhere around tonight. Did you?"

"Come to think of it, no, I didn't. And he's usually around at everything that goes on. He takes that little notebook from his back pocket and starts scribbling. I always josh him and tell him I'll buy him a bigger one for his next birthday. But he calls it his lucky notebook. I don't think you could pry it out of his hand if you had a gun to his head."

Fargo was tugging his clothes on as she spoke. She was wonderfully, gloriously naked as she stood up and came to him. And not self-conscious about it in any way. "I don't suppose you'll be stopping through here again anytime soon."

He took her in his arms. She was so fresh, eager. The temptation to change his mind, to stay came surging through him until he remembered O'Malley. Strange about him not being around tonight. Very strange.

He forced his arms to shed her and strode to the door before he changed his mind.

"I guess I could come back through this way when I'm done seeing my friends."

That great girlish laugh. "You'd better. Or I'll come looking for you."

He went out into the cold harsh night. It was like being banished from Eden.

18

The lobby of O'Malley's hotel bore a sign on an easel noting: RENT BY WEEK, MONTH, YEAR. The Mountainaire had probably been a simple two-story hotel in reasonably good repair a few years earlier. But now there were three other better designed and better constructed hotels. In order to keep its doors open The Mountainaire had likely had to turn itself into a boardinghouse of sorts.

Located at the opposite end of the main street and thus reasonably far away from the celebrating going on in the saloons, the hotel was quiet enough to let the night clerk doze off with a newspaper over his face. Fargo guessed he was the room clerk because he had a large ring of keys on the arm of the lobby sofa where he slept. He must have been a light sleeper, though, Fargo reasoned, because about the time Fargo reached the desk, the newspaper was torn away from the face and the face looked startled. A heavyset man with an unruly red mustache jumped to his feet as if he were standing to military attention.

"Yessir, evening, sir. Business was slow so I—"

"Don't blame you at all. I'd probably do the same thing. I'm looking for Mr. O'Malley. You seen him tonight?"

The clerk, starting to neatly fold the newspaper, said, "Come to think of it, I haven't. Of course I was so caught up in all the excitement—I was standing out on the porch—he might've slipped out without my seeing him. There was quite a crowd on our steps. Our roomers didn't want to get too close to the shooting and such. Things can go wrong with a crowd like that."

"What's his room number?"

The clerk told him. "I can get you the key if you'd like— Mr. Fargo." He smiled. "I don't have to worry about a man with your reputation now, do I?"

Three minutes later Fargo stood outside O'Malley's door. The hallway was filled with the noises of sleep—snoring, coughing, muttering. Fargo pressed his ear to the door, heard nothing. With one hand he inserted the key and turned it. With the other he slowly drew his Colt. One of the rules of survival was never enter a strange, dark room unarmed.

The door wasn't even half opened before he recognized the stench. He eased his way inside and closed the door carefully behind him. The only light was spill from the window, silver light outlining the ancient bulky furniture. And the ancient bulky Irisher sprawled in death on the floor. Fargo recalled the timbre and bullshit majesty of the voice. And the almost child- ish hope and enthusiasm of words. O'Malley would come back, that was O'Malley's theme. O'Malley would be not just good again, he would be great again.

Poor bastard. Poor drunken bastard.

He crossed the room to the man, found the lantern, struck a lucifer. Light bloomed in the room.

There was nothing to be done for O'Malley, of course. When he left, Fargo would notify Pete Rule and have him get somebody to carry the body down so Sarah Friese or one of her assistants could pick it up. The undertaking business was having a very profitable night.

The lantern was on the edge of the desk and the sputtering flame illuminated several pieces of blank paper. The ashtray told him that O'Malley had been working here and working hard. It overflowed with tobacco and cigarette butts.

He thought again of O'Malley's bragging. What if it hadn't been empty boasting? What if he'd really figured out the identity of the killer? And what if he'd been murdered for just that reason? The likely suspect was Tom Cain. He'd been behind the robbery. And he'd killed the three boys, hadn't he? And set up Lenihan? Logically, all those things were of a piece. The hell of it was that Tom Cain had been killed before Fargo had been able to question him at length. So there were still questions that would never be answered.

Fargo lifted three blank pieces of paper and held them close to the light. The Pinkertons had taught him how to look for imprints on what appeared to be unused pages. If the writer had pressed hard enough while writing, the words could be seen on the pages below by shading a pencil over them. He could see that one of the pieces showed evidence of this kind of unintended encryption.

He set the papers on the desk, picked up a pencil and began to shade over the one page that offered some possible usefulness. He felt excited without quite knowing why. Hadn't everything been wrapped up with the death of Tom Cain? Hadn't O'Malley made a lot of enemies in this town and wasn't his murder probably just a coincidence?

But no, that was the part that struck him as impossible. Somebody had killed O'Malley because he had in fact known something about the robbery and killings. Meaning that maybe Cain wasn't the only person involved.

But the Pinkerton trick didn't reveal anything but gibberish. Apparently this page had been used as a second sheet under several pages. At a quick glance all Fargo could see were several layers of words that canceled each other out. He cursed out loud.

There was a small wastebasket next to the desk. He reached down and picked it up. There were several balled-up pieces of paper in it. He went through them quickly. None of them contained anything useful; most seemed to be about other, lesser stories that O'Malley had been working on.

Then Fargo remembered the notebook. The small one that had fit comfortably in the reporter's back pocket. The one that looked as if a child would use it playing journalist. The one that O'Malley referred to as his "lucky" notebook.

He was pretty certain that the killer had taken all the pages from the story O'Malley had been working on. The one that would name names in the robbery and killings. The killer no doubt thought that with O'Malley dead and the story destroyed he would be safe for sure.

But had the killer remembered O'Malley's notebook?

Poor old O'Malley, Fargo thought as he bent down to turn the man on his side. This should have been his big day. The day when he got at least a little of his former self-respect back. The day when fine meals and fine liquor and fine women would have been his again, at least fleetingly. But the killer had put an end to all that.

The notebook was in O'Malley's back pocket. This close to his backside the odor of his befouled trousers was sharp in Fargo's nostrils.

But he had the book. He took it to the desk and dragged the lantern closer. He spent the next five minutes thumbing through the last fifteen pages. Easy to see how O'Malley's interest had gone from suspicion to actually working toward making his case the way a good journalist—or detective— would. The suspicion had been simple enough. He'd started noticing how the suspect's facial expressions changed whenever he was around Amy Peters. This ultimately led to O'Malley breaking into the suspect's place and finding the things stolen from Amy Peters' house during that break-in. The man had developed an obsession with her. He had deluded himself into believing—this was O'Malley's conjecture, anyway—that if he eliminated Ned Lenihan from the picture she would be his. He would also eliminate Tom Cain. Cain actually had been behind the robbery. The suspect had known this from the beginning, having overheard it when Cain had mistakenly thought he was alone in the office talking to one of the boys. Cain might be able to talk himself out of the robbery. But three murders? If he was implicated in them, there was no way the town would let him be. So the suspect killed the boys, knowing he'd blame Tom Cain for the robberies. And would then be able to blame him for the killings, too.

O'Malley had laid all this out neatly in his pocket-sized notebook. Fargo imagined that he had planned on confronting the suspect with this theory and watching the man's face for confirmation. O'Malley made reference to the silver button several times in these pages. Proof that the suspect had indeed broken into Amy Peters' home. And that he was in fact obsessed with her.

But O'Malley was old and slow. It wouldn't have taken much effort on the part of the suspect to realize that O'Malley was closing in on him. And so he'd tracked him here to his room where O'Malley had laid out the story on his desk. The suspect had killed O'Malley and taken the pages.

And now Fargo was going after the suspect, planning to do the world and himself a favor—by killing the son of a bitch.

19

A haze of smoke lay over the interior of the Gold Mine, dirty yellow in the seamy light of the lanterns and Rochester lamps. The men drank and laughed and the saloon girls circulated, making up to men old enough to be their fathers and in some cases their grandfathers. The merry piano music seemed an insult to the cold, somber mountain darkness. Cards were dealt and slapped down. Men trekked out to the latrines dug in back and trekked back blowing into their hands for warmth. Fargo observed all this over the top of the batwings. He stood outside. If anybody had noticed him they hadn't let on.

But they would notice him very soon now.

He pushed through the batwings, leaving the fresh air for the sour smells of beer and smoke and sweat and the stray stark jabs of windblown latrine odors carried on the winds.

Nobody paid him any attention. Not when he was just standing there. Not even when he drew his Colt and pointed it directly at the back of Pete Rule who was standing at the bar having a good time with a couple of cronies. But when the colored piano player finished a song, Fargo spoke up loud enough for the girls and their customers upstairs to hear.

Then everybody noticed.

"Rule, I want you to put your gun down on the bar and slide it up toward the door. Then I want you to turn around and face me while I tell everybody how you killed those three boys and how you killed O'Malley, too, because he figured out you were behind it."

"Hell, Skye, are you drunk? I thought we were friends."

Rule's attempt to make light of the situation would have been more believable if his voice hadn't been shaking so bad.

"You heard what I said, Rule. Your gun on the bar and right now. Unless you want to try and draw on me."

"You sure you know what the hell you're talking about, Mr. Fargo?" the bartender said. "Pete here was the one who figured out that Cain was behind the robbery."

"That's right. Cain was behind the robbery. But not the killings. Rule did those so he could set up Ned Lenihan. He thought that if Lenihan was out of the way he could start courting Amy Peters."

The bartender wasn't the only one who laughed. Half the drinkers joined in. It was harsh, contemptuous laughter. Laughter that said that the idea that Pete Rule would ever have a chance with Amy Peters was downright embarrassing.

Rule still hadn't turned around.

"You hear that, Rule?" Fargo snapped. "You killed four people for nothing. Amy wouldn't ever have anything to do with somebody like you. Especially if she ever found out that you broke into her house and stole some of her things. That's pretty humiliating I'd think, Rule. But you did it." Fargo wasn't usually cruel but he knew what he wanted and cruelty was the quickest way to get it. "You want to tell everybody here what you did with her clothes? You built a little shrine to her, didn't you? Sit there at night and stare at the photographs of her you stole? What kind of a man would do that? Not the kind of man Amy would ever have anything to do with."

His mind and his gun were ready to kill Rule. Eager to kill Rule. But the sound Rule made shocked Fargo and probably shocked everybody else in the saloon. A tortured sob. And hands not going to his gun but to his face. Covering up his shame. Fargo could see only his back but the way his shoulders seemed to collapse and the way Rule seemed to fold in half told the Trailsman that there would be no gunplay now. Fargo's harsh words had destroyed Rule almost as effectively as bullets would have. In other circumstances Fargo might have felt sorry for the man. But no, not ever, not this man.

The men Rule had been laughing with moved away from him as if they'd suddenly learned that he was a plague carrier. The bartender stared at him as if he had just seen the boogeyman he'd heard about all his life. A frozen silence lay on the air.

"I need your gun on the bar, Rule. Now."

Slowly, Rule turned toward him. It was as if he hadn't heard Fargo's command. He didn't make any move toward his gun at all. Even from this distance Fargo could see the tears that streaked the man's face and the gaze that saw beyond Fargo, saw some other realm that only Pete Rule knew.

"I loved her, Fargo."

And then he did it. Even in that instant, even as he fired, Fargo realized that he was helping Rule do what Rule didn't have nerve enough to do alone. As Rule's right hand dropped to his six-shooter and his fingers closed on the handle, Fargo shot him three times in the chest. The crack of the gun was louder than any piano music could ever be and the stench of gunfire stronger even than the stench of the latrine out back.

There was no dramatic death. Rule was thoroughly dead by the time his head cracked against the floor. There was a brief spasm running down the legs and into the feet. Blood began seeping into Rule's shirt.

The bartender said, "Well, I guess we have a lot to thank you for, Mr. Fargo. You sure figured this out for us."

"O'Malley figured it out. Not me." Fargo holstered his gun and started to turn back to the batwings.

"What the hell're we going to do for a sheriff now?" the bartender said.

"That's your problem," Fargo said. "I was going to wait till dawn to get out of this town but I'm not going to wait any longer."

He pushed through the batwings and out into the clarity and beauty of the mountain-shadowed night.

Ten minutes later he was saddling up his big Ovaro stallion. And five minutes after that he was passing the WELCOME TO CAWTHORNE sign.

LOOKING FORWARD!
The following is the opening
section of the next novel in the exciting
Trailsman **series from Signet:**

THE TRAILSMAN #335
RIVERBOAT RAMPAGE

The Missouri River, 1860—
the Big Muddy will run red with blood
when Skye Fargo rides a riverboat to Hell.

Raucous shouting attracted the attention of the big man in buckskins. He looked toward the docks and saw a large group of people gathered around something, blocking his sight of whatever it was. Skye Fargo gave a mental shrug and pointed the big, black-and-white Ovaro stallion toward his destination, a waterfront tavern called Red Mike's.

Then somebody in the crowd behind him let out a whoop and yelled, "Kill him, Owen! Bash the dummy's brains out!"

That prompted a burst of laughter, and somebody else shouted, "He can't do that! The dummy ain't got no brains!"

Fargo reined the Ovaro to a halt. His mouth quirked at the irony.

Then he turned the stallion around and headed back toward the commotion at the docks.

With his buckskins, close-cropped dark beard, and broad-brimmed Stetson, Fargo looked like the veteran frontiersman he was. A long-barreled Colt .44 rode in a holster at his hip, and tucked into a sheath strapped to his right calf was a heavy-bladed Arkansas Toothpick. The butt of a Henry repeater stuck up from a saddle boot. Plenty of men out here went armed. With Skye Fargo, it was like the weapons were part of his body.

He reined in again. Now that he was closer, he could see over the heads of the crowd. The shouting men formed a circle around a couple of hombres who were fighting.

Or rather, one of the men was fighting. The other had his thick, muscular arms raised and his head hunched down as far as it would go between his massive shoulders. He just stood there, absorbing the punishment that his opponent dealt out. The look on his face was one of dull confusion, as if he couldn't understand why the other man was hitting him.

The man doing the punching was big, too, and dressed like one of the dockworkers. He had a thatch of dark hair and a mustache that curled up on the ends. The sleeves of his shirt were rolled up over brawny forearms. The hamlike fists at the ends of those arms shot out again and again, thudding into the body of the younger man.

The spectators kept up their whooping and hollering as they made bets on the outcome. Fargo watched and saw that most of the action seemed to be going through a slender young man who stood to one side, a bowler hat pushed back on his curly, light brown hair. Fargo's lake blue eyes narrowed as his gaze went back and forth between that young man and the one the dockworker was thrashing.

Fargo thought he saw a family resemblance between the two youngsters. Unless he missed his guess, they were brothers.

The massacre—you couldn't really call it a fight—continued for long minutes. The dockworker's fists had opened up several cuts around his opponent's eyes. Blood smeared the young man's face.

One of the spectators cupped his hands around his mouth and yelled, "Finish him off, Owen! This is gettin' boring!"

Grinning, Owen cocked his fists and angled in, poised for the knockout.

The youngster in the bowler hat reached up and tugged on the brim.

The young man who'd been getting pounded finally threw a punch, a slow, ponderous roundhouse right. At least, the blow appeared slow and ponderous at first. But somehow it made its way past Owen's suddenly frantic attempt to block it and exploded on the dockworker's jaw. A collective "Oh!" of shock came from the crowd as Owen went up in the air, his feet rising several inches off the ground before he came crashing back down on the ground. He twitched a couple of times and then lay still, with his eyes rolled back in their sockets.

Silence reigned over the crowd now.

The youngster in the bowler hat rushed over to his brother. "Are you all right, Denny?" he asked anxiously. "Did he hurt you?"

"Nuh . . . no, I reckon I'm all right, Cord," Denny said. "Did I hurt that fella? I didn't mean to hurt him. I just wanted him to stop whalin' on me."

Tears began to run from Denny's eyes and down his moon face.

"I didn't mean to hurt him!" he wailed.

One of the spectators stepped forward and said, "Uh, that's all right, young fella. Don't worry about it. Owen's kind of a mean son of a bitch anyway. He's the one who picked a fight with you."

Denny kept blubbering. Cord reached around his shoulders, or tried to, anyway, and started to lead him away. The crowd parted to let them through.

"It's all right, it's all right," Cord murmured to his brother. "Everybody knows you didn't mean to hurt anybody, Denny."

That just made Denny cry harder. Cord patted him on the back, which was as wide and sturdy as a stone wall.

"Hey, young fella!" one of the spectators called. "You forgot about your money."

Cord looked back, evidently confused. "Money? Oh!" His expression cleared. "The bets."

"Yeah." The man stepped forward and crammed some greenbacks in Cord's hand. "I don't welsh on my bets. That brother o' yours got damned lucky when he landed that punch, but that don't matter. He still won, so I'm payin' off."

"Me, too," another man said. One by one, all the members of the crowd who had bet against Denny gathered around Cord and handed money to him.

"I feel bad about taking this," Cord protested. "Like that fella said, Denny just got lucky. I never dreamed he'd win. The only reason I backed him was family pride, you know. A man can't bet against his own brother."

"No, sir, he sure can't," one of the men agreed. "You should take that brother of yours and get him a good meal. Maybe some licorice candy. That'll make him feel better."

"You know, I think it just might," Cord said. "Thank you."

One of the spectators nudged another and said, "Let's drag Owen over to the water trough and dunk his head. That ought to wake him up."

"Yeah," agreed the other man. He turned to Cord and Denny. "Mister, you and your brother best get on out of here. Owen ain't gonna be happy when he wakes up. He can be a real son of a bitch when he's mad."

"Just like an old grizzly bear," another man said.

Cord nodded. "Thanks. We'll do that. Come on, Denny."

He led Denny down the street, away from the docks. Still seated on the Ovaro at the edge of the crowd, Fargo watched them go.

Then, after a moment, he walked the stallion after them.

Cord and Denny turned a corner, and as soon as they were out of sight of the docks, Cord tugged on his brother's sleeve and started moving faster. Fargo trailed them until they reached a run-down saloon several blocks from the waterfront. They went inside.

Fargo started to turn and ride away, but his curiosity got the better of him. He swung down from the saddle, looped the Ovaro's reins around the hitch rail in front of the saloon, and followed the two youngsters inside. . . .

No other series packs this much heat!

THE TRAILSMAN

**Follow the trail of the gun-slinging heroes of
Penguin's Action Westerns at
penguin.com/actionwesterns**